Nigel Hinton

The Finders

Illustrated by Derek Brazell

VIKING

Published by the Penguin Group
Penguin Books Ltd, 27 Wrights Lane, London w8 5tz, England
Penguin Books USA Inc., 375 Hudson Street, New York 10014, USA
Penguin Books Australia Ltd, Ringwood, Victoria, Australia
Penguin Books Canada Ltd, 10 Alcorn Avenue, Toronto, Ontario, Canada m4v 3b2
Penguin Books (NZ) Ltd, 182–190 Wairau Road, Auckland 10, New Zealand

Penguin Books Ltd, Registered Offices: Harmondsworth, Middlesex, England

First published 1993
1 3 5 7 9 10 8 6 4 2

Text copyright © Nigel Hinton, 1993
Illustrations copyright © Derek Brazell, 1993

The moral right of the author has been asserted

Typeset by Datix International Limited, Bungay, Suffolk
Printed in England by Clays Ltd, St Ives plc

A CIP catalogue record for this book is available from the British Library
ISBN 0–670–84641–4

Chapter One

It all started on a very ordinary day.

As usual, Rosie was the first one to get up and go downstairs. She had just finished laying the table for breakfast when Mark came in, with Jimmy holding his hand. It was what always happened. Just an ordinary day, not at all the sort of day you would expect something amazing to happen.

As usual, Mark was still half asleep and didn't even bother to say hello. He simply sat on his stool, picked up his spoon and stared at his cereal bowl.

Jimmy sat down on the floor. He had been able to walk for over two months, but for some reason he still preferred to crawl first thing in the morning. This morning, as usual, he headed straight for the cat's bowl. Rosie was just about to say, 'No, Jimmy,' when she saw it was empty. It would keep him out of worse trouble for a while. Jimmy reached the cat's bowl, turned it upside-down, pushed it across the lino, then picked it up and put it on his head.

'Flakes or crispies, Mark?' Rosie asked as she stood on a chair and opened the top cupboard.

'I want raisins,' Mark said dreamily.

'But do you want flakes or crispies with them?'

'Yes,' answered Mark.

'Which? Flakes or crispies?' Rosie said patiently.

It was the same routine every morning. She waited while Mark thought.

'Flakes,' he said at last.

'Flakes what?'

'Flakes and raisins.'

'Flakes and raisins what?'

'Flakes and raisins and milk.'

'Flakes and raisins and milk what?' Rosie said, knowing that this was where Mark's game always ended.

'Flakes and raisins and milk, *please*,' Mark said. While Rosie poured the flakes and raisins and milk, Jimmy continued to crawl round the room, pushing the cat's bowl. Rosie bent down and gave him some raisins, but he wasn't hungry because he just put them in the bowl and kept on pushing it round the floor.

She sat down and started eating her breakfast. She had almost finished when Dad came in. He kissed her on the top of her head, ruffled Mark's hair, and tapped Jimmy on his bottom with the newspaper. He cut a slice of bread and was just putting it in the toaster when Mark laughed and pointed.

Jimmy was bent over the cat's bowl, trying to eat the raisins like a cat.

'No, Jimbo, that's dirty,' Dad said, and picked him up. He sniffed. 'Urgh – why is it you always need changing when I'm just about to eat my breakfast? Come on.'

Dad carried Jimmy out and Mark started chanting, 'Pingy, pongy, poo. Dingy, dongy, doo.'

He was still chanting it five minutes later when Dad came back with Jimmy. Dad gave him a look and Mark went silent. He chased a last bit of flake round his bowl with his spoon, then, very quietly, he started to say, 'Pingy, pongy, poo,' again.

'Mark,' Dad said, 'I'm warning you.'

At that moment Mum came in.

'What's he up to?' she asked.

'The usual,' Dad said. 'Driving us all mad with his silly chanting.'

'Oh, Mark, dear,' Mum said. 'Morning, Rosie. Morning, Jimbo.'

Mark pointed his spoon at her.

'Mum and Dad,' he said, then waved the spoon like a magic wand and added, 'Dum and Mad.'

For a moment Dad looked as if he was going to be angry, but then his eyes wrinkled up and he couldn't stop himself laughing.

'Quite right – we've been driven dumb and mad by you. Now get on with your breakfast.'

'I've finished.'

'Right then – get yourself ready for school. And you, Rosie. And help him with his laces if he can't do them.'

'All right,' Rosie said, pushing Mark ahead of her out of the door while he tried to dig his elbows into her ribs.

An ordinary morning. A very ordinary morning.

The usual ordinary things.

Mark couldn't tie his laces and then wouldn't keep his feet still while Rosie tried to help. He got to the bathroom first and left toothpaste dribbling out of the tube as usual. Mrs Taylor came to pick them up as usual. Mum and Dad kissed them goodbye as usual. And they set off for school as usual – Rosie walking with Mrs Taylor while Mark ran on ahead with Andy, Mrs Taylor's son.

It seemed the most normal, ordinary day possible. But all that was just about to change.

Chapter Two

The morning was bright and sunny as they crossed the park. The green grass glowed in the sunlight and the light breeze shook the red and golden leaves on the autumn trees. A large bumble-bee flew up from a late rose and seemed almost too heavy to keep itself in the air. It bobbed slowly in front of Rosie, then disappeared into the bushes.

'Do bees have hearts, Mrs Taylor?' Rosie asked.

'I expect so,' Mrs Taylor said. Then a couple of moments later she said, 'Perhaps they don't. I don't know. What a funny question.'

She looked very puzzled as they walked on and Rosie thought she was going to say something else about bees, but she suddenly pointed at the two boys, who were running out through the gate on the other side of the park.

'Andy! Mark! Wait!' she shouted, but they disappeared through the exit.

Mrs Taylor gave a little shriek and started to run and Rosie ran after her. When they got to the gate they found the boys sitting on the wall outside, waiting for them.

'Don't you ever do that again,' Mrs Taylor

puffed. 'You gave me a terrible scare.'

The boys gave each other a cheeky look, then jumped off the wall and strolled away down the road with Mrs Taylor after them. Rosie was just about to follow when she noticed that one of her shoe-laces was undone. She knelt down to tie it up, and that was when it happened.

When she bent down he wasn't there, but when she stood up again he was.

An old man.

As if he had come out of nowhere.

His hair was white, his face was as red as a lobster and his whole body was trembling as he bent forward on his walking-stick. His pale-blue eyes stared at her – so very pale and cloudy that they looked like blind eyes.

'I'm sorry to bother you,' he said, 'but I wonder if you could do me a favour?'

Rosie looked along the road. Mrs Taylor and the boys were already a long way away. She knew she shouldn't talk to strangers, but surely this old man couldn't hurt her?

'I've got this little present,' the old man said, holding out a small parcel wrapped in brown paper. It was about the size of a small book. 'It's for my brother's birthday. I want to send it, but it's a long way for me to go to the letter-box – my legs are too old and feeble.'

'I'll post it for you,' Rosie said, and held out her hand.

'Just one thing,' the man said, pulling the parcel

away. 'It's Friday today, isn't it?'

Rosie nodded.

'Well, his birthday is on Monday, so I don't want it posted today. Just slip it into your school-bag and leave it there – it's not too big. Then if you post it tomorrow, he'll get it on Monday morning – it'll be much nicer if it turns up *on* his birthday. Will you do that for me?'

'Yes,' Rosie said.

'There's a kind girl.'

He held the parcel out. His hand was shaking. Rosie looked at him. His lips were smiling, but his eyes were fierce and seemed to be ordering her. She reached for the parcel.

As her hand closed on it, a tingle shot up her arms, along her shoulders, up her neck, and into

her head. For a moment a bright star-shape flicked from one side of her brain to the other and then it was gone. It happened so quickly that she couldn't be sure it had happened at all.

She put the parcel in her school-bag and, almost as if she were repeating an order, she found herself saying, 'I'll keep it there. I won't let anyone see it and I'll post it tomorrow morning.'

'There's a good girl,' said the old man. 'You'd better run along and catch up with the others.'

Rosie ran fast after Mrs Taylor and Andy and Mark. She wanted to be with them and, somehow, she wanted to get away from the man. The strange thing was that she quickly caught up with Mrs Taylor and the boys, but she didn't feel as if she had got away from the man at all. It was as if he was still there with her.

She turned round, but he was nowhere to be seen.

Chapter Three

Rosie was in big trouble all day. She just couldn't help it – everything she said or did was wrong. Mr Bignell was walking across the playground when she arrived and he smiled and said, 'Morning, Rosie.'

Before she could stop herself, she called him by his nickname.

'Morning, Mr Big Nose.'

Mr Bignell looked at her in surprise and said, 'Don't be so cheeky.'

She managed to say, 'Sorry, Mr Bignell,' but it was a hard job not to call him 'Big Nose' again.

Then during assembly she found everything funny and had to stop herself giggling all the time. When it came to the hymn, it was her favourite – 'Morning Has Broken' – but while everyone else was singing the proper words, she sang:

Morning has broken,
So has the saucer,
Parrot keeps saying
Teacher is mad.

During Maths she spent her time writing PLEASE KICK ME in big letters on a piece of paper. Then she stuck the paper on the back of the boy in front. He got kicked constantly during playtime and didn't understand why.

In the lesson before lunch-time she wrote a note and passed it round the class. The note had the name Trudie Roberts on it, and the message was: I love you. Please kiss me in the corridor at lunch. Stephen Edwards.

Stephen was a shy little boy and Trudie was a large girl with long hair who was always talking about boys. All the boys hated her.

Rosie watched as the note was handed from person to person and finally arrived at Trudie. She opened the note and Rosie almost burst out laughing as she saw Trudie turn round and look at Stephen with big moony eyes.

At the end of the lesson Rosie stood in the corridor and watched as Trudie waited by the door. When Stephen came out with one of his friends she put her big tubby hand on the little boy's shoulder.

'Hello,' Trudie said.

Stephen looked at her, surprised.

'I love you too,' she said, and bent down and kissed him right on the lips.

Stephen looked as if a pig had wiped its slimy snout across his mouth.

'Urgghhh!' he shouted, and ran off down the corridor towards the boys' toilets as if he was going to be sick.

All afternoon Rosie found it hard to concentrate

and she stared out of the window, her head filled with strange thoughts.

A huge crow flapped lazily from a distant tree and landed on the playground just outside the window. He walked up and down a couple of times, his glossy feathers shining in the sunlight and his black eyes looking like cold jewels.

Then from round the corner of the school came a large grey cat. Rosie expected the crow to fly away but it stood still and let the cat pad slowly right up to it. Suddenly the two of them turned and looked directly at her.

'Rosie Brooks!' shouted Mr Bignell.

'Yes, sir,' she said, jumping in surprise.

'Get on with your work. I really don't know

what's got into you today.'

'Sorry, sir,' she said, and began working on the map that everyone else was drawing.

She didn't dare stop work for about ten minutes, but she couldn't help thinking about the crow and the cat. Finally she saw that Mr Bignell had his back to her, so she took a quick peep out of the window. The playground was empty – the cat and the crow had gone.

She bent down to start work on the map again and could hardly believe her eyes.

Instead of a proper map of Australia, she had drawn what looked like a pirate's treasure map. Instead of proper names like Sydney and Melbourne, she had written names like Dead Man's Cove, Murder Point and Blood Bay. And underneath she had drawn a big skull and cross-bones. How could she have done all that without knowing what she was doing?

It was scary.

The skull grinned up at her and Rosie shivered.

Chapter Four

Things were just as bad when she got home. She teased Mark, she teased Jimmy and she even teased the cat.

Mark just told her to go and boil her head. And Freddie the cat got fed up with having his tail pulled, so he turned round and dug his claws into her hand. But when she took Jimmy's toy truck away from him he started to cry and Mum came in and told her off.

'Really, Rosie, you're a little devil today. I don't know what's got into you.'

That was the second time someone had said that, and Rosie knew it was true because she couldn't understand it herself. What *had* got into her? Part of her was saying, 'Stop all this – it's horrible,' but another part of her just wouldn't stop.

She made up her mind to stop letting the horrible part of her win. She went to Mark's room and tried to make it up with him, but he was busy drawing, and this time he told her not only to go and boil her head but to eat it as well.

'How can I eat my own head, stupid?' she said spitefully, as the horrible part of her bubbled up again.

'Your mouth is big enough to eat anything,' Mark said, and went on drawing.

Jimmy soon forgave her, though, and she took him for a ride round the garden in his push-chair. He loved being pushed fast and she nearly wore herself out running up and down to please him.

''Gain,' he shouted whenever she stopped for breath.

'One last go,' she finally said, and charged down the path towards the end of the garden. Jimmy shrieked and laughed as they juddered to a stop a few centimetres away from the end wall.

Suddenly Rosie had a terrible shock. A big black crow landed on top of the wall and a moment later a grey cat leaped up and sat down next to it. They put their heads together and stared at her.

A cold shiver ran all the way down from her neck to her feet. She managed to stop herself from screaming because she didn't want to scare Jimmy, but she backed quickly down the path, pulling the push-chair after her, while the crow and the cat watched.

As soon as she got indoors she ran and told her mum.

'I don't see why you're making such a fuss about a cat and a bird,' Mum said. 'They can't hurt you.'

'But it's the same ones I saw at school, Mum. They give me the creeps.'

'Oh, come on, it's just a coincidence – nothing to worry about,' Mum said, giving her a hug. 'Just forget it and fetch Jimmy out of the push-chair. Tea's ready.'

Rosie tried to forget, but as soon as tea was over she ran to the back door and looked out. The wall was empty but she had a horrible feeling that the cat and the crow weren't very far away. She tried to read, she tried to watch TV and she tried to practise her recorder, but she couldn't stop thinking about the cat and the crow. Finally it was time to go to bed.

She had just got into her pyjamas when she suddenly remembered the old man and the parcel he'd given her. There it was, tucked down in her school-bag under her pencil-case. As her fingers touched it, there was a blinding flash from outside, followed almost at once by a huge crack of thunder

that shook the whole house. She rushed to the window.

Dark black clouds were rolling across the sky. There was another flash of lightning and, as the silver streak zigzagged across the sky, she saw the cat and the crow. They were sitting on the lawn looking straight up at her. She quickly closed the curtains, jumped into bed and pulled the covers up over her head.

All night she had strange and scary dreams. She wanted to wake up but she couldn't. Instead, she kept dreaming about a dark house where dead animals lurked in the shadows. And all the time she had the feeling that someone was after her and that no matter how fast she ran she wouldn't be able to get away.

At last it was morning. She woke up and the dreams were over, but the feeling was still there. Even with the light coming through the window, even with the normal everyday sounds of the house around her, Rosie felt that something awful was just about to happen.

Chapter Five

'I've packed your rucksack,' Mum said at break-fast.

It took Rosie a moment to realize what she was talking about. Of course! Mum and Dad and the two boys were going to visit Grandma for the weekend and Rosie was going to stay with Rebecca.

Everything had been so strange since yesterday that she had forgotten all about it. Great! She loved staying at Rebecca's house – they always had so much fun. It would be just the thing to help her forget all those dreams.

She ran upstairs to get ready. At the last minute she remembered the old man's parcel and slipped it into the rucksack.

'Mum, Dad's going to be ages packing the car – can I walk round to Rebecca's on my own? It's not far,' she added when her mum looked doubtful.

'Oh, all right, but go straight there – promise?'

Rosie nodded, but crossed her fingers behind her back because she'd have to go a bit out of her way to post the parcel.

'Right then, off you go,' her mum said, giving her a hug. 'Have a lovely time. And we'll see you tomorrow about tea-time.'

'Give my love to Grandma,' Rosie called as she set off down the path.

'Urmphh!' Dad grunted as he struggled to fit Jimmy's cot into the back of the car.

'Bye, Rosie,' shouted Mark, then unexpectedly he ran after her and asked for a kiss.

She bent down and kissed him on the cheek. For some reason she suddenly felt sad. It was almost as if she was saying goodbye for ever.

She wanted to turn back and go with them to Grandma's, but something inside her told her she couldn't. She just patted Mark on the top of his head where a tuft of hair always stood up no matter how hard you tried to brush it or press it down. He smiled at her, then she walked away down the road.

She turned left into Wolmark Road and then, instead of going straight on towards Rebecca's house, she turned right into Frankley Avenue. It was a quiet street with all the houses set back and hidden behind tall hedges. There was nobody about and there was a kind of hush in the air.

She walked fast towards the post-box and as she got nearer she pulled the parcel out of the rucksack. The parcel seemed warm and it made her hand tingle. Ever since the old man had given it to her, things had gone wrong. She didn't know why, but she couldn't wait to get rid of this mysterious box wrapped in brown paper.

She reached the post-box, took one last look at the parcel, then dropped it through the hole.

At once the tingling stopped and it was as if a heavy load had been lifted off her. She felt like skipping and running for joy all the way to Rebecca's house, but as she turned she saw a movement across the road.

Was that a grey cat that had just slipped behind the hedge? And was that a crow crouched on the chimney over there?

Before she had a chance to look closer, everything went dark as something was pulled over her head. She started to scream, but as she opened her mouth she found it filled with rough sack. Then a strong pair of hands grabbed her shoulders and pushed, while another pair of hands grabbed her wrists and pulled.

Chapter Six

The hands pulled and pushed and Rosie blindly stumbled the way they led her. When she tried to stop, the hands pulled and pushed even harder, and when she tried to shout, 'Help!' the sack filled her mouth so that no sound came out.

After a few moments a door creaked open and the hands pushed her forward. Then the door creaked closed behind her.

There was a long, long silence. Where was she? Was she alone or were the two people still there? What was going to happen? She held her breath and waited.

Suddenly a high, squeaky voice in front of her said, 'Mr Ikbal, sir . . .'

'What is it, lad?' a very gruff voice behind her asked.

'Is everything all right?' squeaked the high voice.

'Of course it is. All according to plan,' said the gruff voice. 'Now we must just wait patiently until midnight to take her across.'

Rosie was astonished. These voices didn't sound like kidnappers. The high one sounded almost like a young boy and although the deep one was very gruff it didn't sound at all cruel. She opened her mouth to speak but the sack went into it again and her words came out as a mumble. She shook her head to try to get the sack out.

'Mr Ikbal,' whispered the high voice, 'she's growling at us. I don't like it here.'

'Now just be brave, Sidri. She won't hurt us. I'll make the formal arrest now,' the deep voice said. There was a little cough as he cleared his throat, then he went on, 'My name is Ikbal. I arrest you in my name; in the name of my young apprentice, Sidri, and in the ninety-nine names of goodness. You have been captured and we will take you back to where you belong.'

Rosie could hardly believe her ears. Arrested? These people must be policemen. It must all be a mistake. She tried to speak but again the sack got in the way and the words came out all mumbly.

'Mr Ikbal, I . . . I'm scared,' said Sidri and then burst into tears.

'There, there, don't cry,' said Mr Ikbal, but the crying grew louder and turned into sobs.

Rosie didn't understand why, but the sound of crying made her realize how frightened and shocked she was and, before she knew what was happening, she burst into tears too.

'Oh dear, now you've set the Djinn off,' said Mr Ikbal. 'H'm – it must be a trick – I've never heard a Djinn cry before.'

Rosie didn't know what a Djinn was but it didn't sound very nice and it made her cry even more. She sobbed so hard that the sack got caught in her mouth and she began to cough as well, making the most terrible noise.

'Now, stop that at once,' Mr Ikbal said gruffly.

But Rosie couldn't stop.

'Oh dear me, you'll choke if you go on like that. Now, listen. I'll take the sack off your head, but don't try any of your tricks.'

Rosie felt the sack being pulled off her head. She opened her eyes and what she saw made her stop crying at once. She blinked and looked again. It was true.

There was nobody there.

She was standing in an empty garage.

There were a few patches of oil on the floor, a shelf with some tools on it, and an old broom in

26

the corner. There was no sign of the kidnappers and nowhere for them to be hiding.

She blinked again, to make sure.

Nothing. Nobody. Just an empty garage.

'I must be dreaming,' she said out loud.

She said it, but she didn't believe it. Dreams could seem very real but this was just too real. She could smell the stale petrol fumes, she could feel the cold draught blowing under the door and she still had the nasty taste of the sack in her mouth. Then the voices came again and she knew she wasn't dreaming.

'She can't see us, Mr Ikbal,' squeaked the high voice.

'Nonsense, she's trying to trick us. Just watch her blink when I do this.'

Rosie felt a slight puff of wind as if someone was waving a hand in front of her face.

'She didn't blink, Mr Ikbal. She can't see us. That means she's not a Djinn.'

'Of course she is. She's got the smell of magic all over her.'

There was another puff of wind across Rosie's face, then Mr Ikbal's voice came again. And this time there was a note of doubt in it.

'But I must say she doesn't seem to be able to see my hand. And in all my years I've never seen a Djinn cry.'

'She doesn't look like a Djinn, sir.'

'Now, Sidri, how often have I told you that they can take any shape they like? That's the first rule for a Finder to learn. Quiet, gentle old ladies; good-looking heroes; sweet, beautiful young women; fierce old men. Djinn can make themselves look like any of them.'

Rosie had been listening amazed to these voices that came out of thin air, but when she heard the words 'fierce old men' all this mad talk suddenly made sense.

'It's a mistake,' she shouted, and there was a little squeak of surprise from in front of her. 'You've got the wrong person. I'm not a Djinn. But I think I met one the other day. He was very old and he seemed kind, but when I looked in his eyes they were all fierce, as if he was giving me orders. That's what reminded me, when you said "fierce old men". So there's been a mistake, you see.'

All this poured out so fast that Rosie was out of breath when she finished. And it was only at the end that she felt rather silly talking to people she couldn't see. She felt even sillier when nobody replied.

'Are you still here?' she asked, looking round the garage.

There was another long silence, then she heard whispering in the far corner. She waited. The whispering stopped and Mr Ikbal's gruff voice came again.

'Tell me, young girl – and no tricks now – did this man give you anything?'

'Yes,' shouted Rosie. 'He gave me a parcel to

post. And when he gave it to me I felt all funny and since then everything's gone wrong. And I wish I'd never seen him.'

'Oh dear, oh dear,' Mr Ikbal said. 'That must be it then, Sidri. The Djinn knew we were catching up with him and he passed the Djinn Star to her to make us lose his trail. Tell me, young girl, how long did you keep this parcel?'

'He gave it to me yesterday and I posted it this morning,' Rosie said, glad that they seemed to believe her. 'It's all a mistake, you see. Now you can go off and catch him.'

'I'm afraid it's not quite as easy as that,' said Mr Ikbal, sounding less and less gruff and more and more worried. 'We won't be able to catch him until he gets the Djinn Star again. That's not such a big problem because he probably put his own address on that parcel, so we can catch him when he gets it back. But I'm afraid there's a bigger problem.'

'What's that?' Rosie asked.

'You.'

'What do you mean?' Rosie said, suddenly feeling very scared.

'Well, I don't quite know how to say this but . . . you had the Djinn Star for over a day and that means . . .'

Mr Ikbal stopped and cleared his throat, but before he could speak again Sidri's high voice squeaked out, 'It means she's going to be a Djinn too, doesn't it, sir?'

Chapter Seven

Rosie opened her mouth to say something but nothing came out. She was so confused she didn't know whether to be angry or to cry. She just stood there, opening and closing her mouth like the goldfish that Mr Bignell kept in a tank in the classroom.

'What's your name, my dear?' Mr Ikbal asked gently.

'Rosie,' she said, finding her voice at last.

'You'll have to forgive young Sidri, Rosie,' Mr Ikbal went on. 'He's rather new to the job and he tends to say things without thinking. But I'm afraid that what he said is true. The Djinn Star is very powerful. Anyone who keeps it overnight starts to become a Djinn.'

'You're just teasing me, aren't you?' Rosie said hopefully. 'I've never even heard of these Djinn things.'

'They are sometimes called Genii,' Mr Ikbal said.

'Genii,' Rosie laughed, sure now that the whole thing was a joke. 'Those things that appear when people rub magic lamps? They're not real. They're just silly things in stories.'

'Just because they are in stories doesn't mean they aren't true,' Mr Ikbal said. 'But you are quite right, there are no such things as Genii in bottles or in lamps. However, real Djinn do exist and they are some of the wickedest creatures in the whole of creation.'

His voice was so serious and yet so calm that Rosie knew he was telling the truth. She shivered. It sounded ridiculous and she didn't understand it, but she believed him.

'And you think I'm turning into one?' she asked in a whisper.

'I'm afraid so,' Mr Ikbal replied. 'You said that you already felt . . . er . . . funny and that things had gone wrong. What did you mean?'

Rosie told them everything. The tingling, the star-shape light in her brain, the bad things she'd done, the strange map, the crow, the cat, the storm. Everything she could think of.

'Oh dear,' Mr Ikbal said in his deep voice. 'A cat, a crow – both animals that are attracted to Djinn. Yes, all the signs are there. And I suppose you've started to fly too?'

'Of course not,' Rosie said, and she started to laugh at the silly idea. But her laugh was cut short as she felt herself begin to rise slowly into the air. It was only a few centimetres but, when she looked down, her feet were definitely no longer touching the ground.

'Oh help,' she screamed.

She waved her arms to push herself back to the ground and, to her complete surprise, started skimming towards the wall as if she was sliding across ice. She raised her arms to stop herself bumping into the wall and felt herself begin to tip over backwards. She kicked her legs to try to keep herself upright, but the sudden movement made her flip, head over heels, in the air.

'Help!' she shouted again as she found herself upside-down with her head about ten centimetres off the ground.

'Hold on,' Mr Ikbal said and she felt two hands grab her shoulders and turn her the right way up again. But she was still floating in the air.

'How can I get down?' she asked.

'Try wishing with all your might. I don't think you've fully turned into a Djinn yet. So if you think of something honest and kind and loving it might keep the bad side of you at bay.'

Rosie wished hard and tried to think of something good. But the more she tried, the more her mind was filled with horrible ideas. She thought of treading on ants, and she thought of cruel things to say to people and nasty tricks to play on them.

'I can't,' she cried, and started to rise nearer and nearer the ceiling.

'Yes you can, Wosie,' squeaked the high voice of Sidri.

The sound of his babyish voice made Rosie think of Mark. He used to call her 'Wosie' when he first started to talk and it always made her laugh. As soon as she thought of Mark she remembered that moment earlier this morning when he had run after her and asked for a kiss.

In her mind she could see her young brother's face clearly. His long, long eyelashes and his cheeky smile. With a rush in her heart she realized how very much she loved him.

There was a little bump and she found herself standing on the ground again.

'You've done it,' Mr Ikbal said. 'Well done.'

'That means she's not a Djinn yet, doesn't it?' squeaked Sidri excitedly.

'Yes, it does. You must be a very strong young girl, Rosie. Most people are taken over by the power of the Djinn Star in one night. So if we act fast we might be able to help you. But you must try not to fly or think bad thoughts – both of those things will turn you into a Djinn more quickly. And we must get that Star back to its proper owner before it's too late.'

'When would it be too late?' Rosie asked, as a little chill ran up and down her back.

'Well, my dear, even *you* couldn't resist the power of the Djinn Star for another night, so it would have to be placed into the Djinn's hand before the Witching Hour. One minute later and I'm afraid you'll be lost for ever.'

'When's the Witching Hour?' Rosie whispered, feeling her eyes fill with tears.

'Midnight.'

Suddenly it all seemed so hopeless and the tears began to slide down Rosie's cheeks.

'Come on, my dear, don't cry. There's hope yet.'

'But I haven't got the Star,' Rosie sniffed. 'And I don't know where this Djinn is, and even if I find him he's never going to take the Star back, is he?'

'Now, now – never say die,' Mr Ikbal said. 'And always take things one step at a time. First, let's find the Star. What have you done with the parcel?'

'I put it in a post-box down the road.'

'Then let us not waste any time – we must go and get it.'

There was a breeze as something invisible went past her, then the garage door opened and Rosie blinked as the bright sunlight poured in.

Sidri's voice squeaked from outside, 'Come on, Wosie. We've got to go quickly.'

Rosie ran out into the sunlight and her heart was filled with hope. Perhaps it would be all right after all.

She was just about to ask where the Finders were when she bumped into something soft and furry. There was a huge gasp of 'Ooouuf!' followed by a squeaky giggle.

'Oh dear, what have I done?' she asked.

'You knocked all the puff out of Mr Ikbal,' laughed Sidri.

'Sorry,' she said. 'I didn't see you.'

'That's all right,' said Mr Ikbal. 'But perhaps it will be safer if you run ahead and we follow. That way there won't be any painful accidents. Quick now.'

Rosie ran down the road as fast as she could. When she turned the corner into Frankley Avenue her heart sank. The postman was collecting the letters from the box.

'Oh no,' she shouted. 'Wait a minute.'

But the postman was too far away to hear.

She ran as fast as her legs would carry her. She saw the postman put the keys in his pocket. She saw him pick up the bag. She saw him walk towards his van.

'Wait! Wait!' she cried.

She was close enough to make out the number 206 painted on the back door of the van and she could see that the postman had a big bushy beard. She saw him get into the driver's seat.

'No!' she yelled.

There was a puff of smoke as the engine started. The van pulled out from the kerb and set off quickly down the road. It flashed its light and turned left into another road.

By the time Rosie got to the corner the van had disappeared, taking the Djinn Star with it.

Chapter Eight

If she had been on her own, Rosie would probably have given up there and then, but luckily the Finders were there to keep her going.

'Where will he go next?' Mr Ikbal asked.

'To get letters from other boxes and then back to the sorting office,' she said.

'Then we'll go there and wait for him,' said Mr Ikbal. 'Lead the way – but not too fast. Young Sidri's legs aren't used to this running business and mine are getting rather too old for it all.'

It was very strange walking along talking to people she couldn't see, but there were so many things she wanted to ask that Rosie didn't care if some of the passers-by gave her odd looks.

'Are you policemen?' was her first question.

Sidri burst out laughing and he laughed so much that they had to stop walking for a moment before they could go on.

'We're not exactly policemen,' Mr Ikbal said. 'We're called Finders. Our job is to search out Djinn that have come over into this world to do their mischief. When we find them we take them back to the other side. I've been doing it for many, many long years, but this is Sidri's first mission.

I'm supposed to be showing him how it's done, but I'm afraid I'm not doing a very good job at the moment.'

'Yes, you are, sir. I've learned lots and lots.'

This seemed to please Mr Ikbal, because there was a happy chuckle. Rosie could imagine him smiling at his little helper and she wondered what they looked like.

'Why are you invisible?' Rosie asked.

'We're not!' squeaked Sidri, as if he was upset by the idea. Then he added, in a worried tone, 'We're not, are we, sir?'

'Only to human beings,' Mr Ikbal said. 'We can see each other, Djinn can see us – all sorts of creatures can see us. Your eyes and ears can only see and hear certain things. Just think how dogs can hear sounds that you can't, and cats can see things at night that you can't. I always feel sorry for humans because they have such limited senses.'

'Aren't you human beings, then?'

'Oh, my dear, of course not,' Mr Ikbal said, as if the very idea was funny. 'We are angels.'

This time it was Rosie who had to stop walking for a moment.

'Angels?' she gasped.

'That's right. Now, come along – we can't waste time standing here. Let's hold hands and get to this sorting office as fast as possible.'

Rosie felt a large furry hand take one of her hands and a small furry hand take the other. She didn't know whether to scream or laugh or to try

38

to get away from these invisible Finders who said they were angels.

But she didn't do any of these things because the little hand squeezed her hand gently and Sidri's voice said, 'Come on, Wosie – I want to try running again.'

And run they did, all the way to the High Street, where they had to slow down because there were so many shoppers on the pavement.

'Better let go of our hands now,' puffed Mr Ikbal. 'We'll walk just behind you, so that people don't bump into us.'

When they got to the sorting office they watched as postmen went in and out of the building, carrying sacks of mail. There was a line of vans parked in the yard, but number 206 wasn't there.

While they were waiting for it to arrive, Rosie noticed a phone-box across the road, so she dashed over and quickly rang Rebecca. She explained to her friend that the plans had been changed at the last minute and that she wouldn't be able to stay with her for the weekend. Rebecca was disappointed, but said she understood.

Just as Rosie put the phone down she saw van 206 turn into the yard. She ran back across the road and stopped the postman with the big bushy beard just as he was getting out.

'Of course you can't,' he snapped, when she asked if she could have the parcel back. 'Are you stupid or what? How do I know it's yours? Once something has been posted it has to be delivered.'

And before she could think of anything else to say he picked the sacks out of the van and walked into the sorting office.

She peeped through the swing-doors and watched him walk down a ramp to a large area where other postmen and women were busily sorting the mail. She saw him put the sacks down next to a trolley and go across to talk to someone sitting at a desk on the far side of the room.

Now, if she could creep down to the sacks and find the parcel while the postman wasn't looking . . .

Mr Ikbal must have known what she was thinking because he whispered in her ear, 'Everybody is busy and if anybody sees you Sidri and I will be there to help you. I'd go myself, but I don't know what the parcel looks like. It's the only way, my dear.'

Rosie pushed the door wider and stepped inside. The door squeaked loudly but the postmen and women were too busy to notice. She ducked low and tiptoed down the ramp. Just as she reached the bottom she saw the postman with the bushy beard turn and head back towards her. She dived behind the trolley.

Had he seen her? She bent low to peer under the trolley and saw his legs coming closer. Closer. Closer.

He must have seen her.

Suddenly he stopped walking and she saw his

hand reach down and pick up one of the sacks. He turned and walked away towards a bench. Rosie peeped over the top of the trolley and she saw him lift the sack and tip the letters out on to the bench. No parcels. So the parcel with the Djinn Star must be in one of the other two sacks.

She would have to chance it. She looked round – nobody was looking. Now!

She dashed round the trolley and quickly opened the first sack. There seemed to be only letters but she thrust her hand down amongst them and felt.

Letters. Letters. Letters. No parcel.

It must be in the other one.

She glanced round. Bushy Beard was feeding letters into a machine and no one else was looking in her direction. Quick!

She opened the other sack. All she could see was letters again. Perhaps he had already sorted the parcels and left them somewhere else. She pushed her hand down into the letters to make sure. Wait a minute – there was something down near the bottom. A parcel.

It felt the right size but was it the right one? She pulled it out. Yes. She even felt the same tingle shoot up her arm again.

A shadow fell across the parcel and a hand grabbed it from her. It was Bushy Beard.

'What are you doing? I told you outside . . . You're stealing Royal Mail. You're going to have to see my boss about this.'

He took hold of her arm and pulled her towards

a lady sitting at one of the desks. Rosie was just about to try to break free when there were shouts and screams from all over the room. Bushy Beard stopped and turned.

Everybody was staring at the middle of the room, where two sacks of letters were floating through the air and a trolley was whizzing round and round on its own. Suddenly the trolley stopped and the letters piled in it began to shoot up into the air like a fountain.

Rosie realized it must be Mr Ikbal and Sidri, but the postmen and women didn't have the least idea what was happening. They had all turned pale and their mouths were open in shock.

For a moment none of them moved, then a man screamed, 'Ghosts!' and complete panic broke out.

A couple of men tried to climb the wall. Another man dived headlong into a trolley which sped across the room, crashed into a bench, and tipped him out again.

Then everyone bolted towards the exits, bumping and pushing each other to try to be first out.

All except Bushy Beard. His eyes were wide open and his beard was shaking with fright but he held on to Rosie and stood still as if rooted to the spot. In no time at all the other people had burst through the doors and Rosie and Bushy Beard were left alone.

At once the parcels and letters stopped flying through the air and the trolley stopped whizzing round and round. Bushy Beard started to relax, but the next moment he tensed up again.

All the sorting machines stopped working and the room was suddenly very, very quiet. Much too quiet for the postman. He backed up against the wall, pulling Rosie with him.

'Hello? Is anybody there?' he asked in a scared voice.

There was no reply – just an eerie silence that made even Rosie feel uneasy. What would Mr Ikbal and Sidri do next? She didn't have to wait long to find out.

'Whoooah!' shrieked Bushy Beard, letting go of Rosie and crossing his arms over his chest. 'No! Ooh! Ha ha! Nooo-oooahaha-ohaoohaha. No tickles. Ooh no.'

He began whirling round, trying to protect himself – first his neck, now his chin, then under his arms, and then his tummy – as Mr Ikbal and Sidri's invisible hands tickled and prodded him.

'Ahahahaha! Ooh no I can't . . . ooh please . . . I can't . . . stand it . . . ooh haha. No, stop ahahaha.'

He fell to his knees, laughing and whooping, and then began to roll all over the floor, trying to get away.

He dropped the parcel and Rosie darted across and picked it up. Then, while he continued to wriggle and giggle and squeak, she ran up the ramp to the door.

Everything was going to be all right. She was free and she had the parcel.

Her feeling of joy lasted exactly ten seconds. Then it stopped.

Chapter Nine

Rosie burst out of the door into the yard and came face to face with all the postmen and women who had run out there too.

They stepped back a pace, as if they were scared that something horrible might follow her out of the door. She stopped running and smiled at them. They were still all so shocked that they just stared as she slipped the parcel in her rucksack and walked towards the gates. The lady who had been sitting behind the desk opened her mouth to say something, but Rosie kept smiling sweetly and walked right past her.

She had just reached the gates when she heard the doors of the sorting office crash open.

Bushy Beard staggered out into the yard and yelled, 'Get her! She's stolen a parcel.'

He started to run towards her and all the others followed. Rosie turned and raced away towards the High Street

There were shouts of 'Stop her!' from the post-men, and some of the shoppers turned to look, but she sped past them before they could do anything. She glanced over her shoulder and saw two of the leading postmen trip over a dog's lead. A whole group of the others went sprawling on top of them.

Old Bushy Beard managed to dodge out into the road, though, and Rosie could hear the stamp of his boots as he got nearer. Her only hope was to give him the slip.

She dashed through the door of the nearest shop. There was a line of dresses hanging on a rail just inside the door and she ducked behind it and stood stock-still.

The shop was enormous. The first half was a clothes department, then there was an area of flowers and plants, and beyond that was a food section. At the very back of the shop was an escalator taking people up to the second floor, and next to that was a door marked EXIT. If she could get out by that door, without being seen, she would be safe.

She peeped out. Oh no! Bushy Beard was standing a couple of metres away, scanning the crowds for a sign of her. He must have seen her come in. Well, it was no good staying here – she must move while he had his back to her.

She darted out from behind the dresses and began to make her way through the shop, crouching low behind counters and displays of clothes. She was almost at the plant section when she suddenly saw Bushy Beard heading straight towards the counter where she was hiding. She looked round and saw a curtain near her, so she gently pulled it aside and slipped behind it.

It was only when she turned round that she

realized where she was – it was the men's changing-room.

A very fat man in red boxer-shorts was just putting his leg into a pair of trousers. He saw Rosie and tried to pull up the trousers so fast that his feet got tangled in the trouser leg. He hopped up and down to free his feet, stumbled, and fell over in a heap.

'Get out of here! This is for men!' he shouted, his face going as red as his boxer-shorts. 'Get out!'

The man was shouting so loudly that Rosie knew Bushy Beard must have heard and, sure enough, when she dashed out from behind the curtain, there he was. He made a grab for her, but she was too quick for him and she scampered away down the aisle towards the food section.

She dodged in and out of the long line of freezers, and when she looked back she could see that Bushy Beard was puffing badly. If she could just keep going she would soon lose him outside.

She reached the back of the shop, dived down the stairs, and burst through the exit. She was in a narrow alley. To her left was a car-park, in front of her was a tall wall, and to the right was the High Street.

Which way?

She chose the High Street and began running up the slope towards it. She got to the end of the alley and peered out. Some postmen were running along the pavement. She ducked back into the alley and pressed herself against the wall. Four of them ran past but the fifth glanced down the alley and spotted her. He skidded to a halt and called to the others.

Rosie turned and ran back the way she had come. Behind her she could hear the stamp of boots as the postmen began to charge down the alley after her. They were still some way behind, though, so if she could just get to the car-park . . .

Oh no. The shop door swung open and Bushy Beard limped out of the exit and stood in the middle of the alley. She was trapped. Bushy Beard ahead, the other postmen behind. She looked at the wall, but it was much too high to climb. Oh, if only she could fly.

Of course – *fly!* She was nearly a Djinn, wasn't she? She could fly, couldn't she? She'd done it this morning. Well, do it now.

The postmen and Bushy Beard were getting closer. Quick! *Fly!*

She clenched her teeth and tried to force herself into the air. Nothing. She jumped as high as she could into the air but only thudded back to the ground again.

The postmen and Bushy Beard were getting closer.

Mr Ikbal had made her think good thoughts to bring her back to the ground, so if she tried thinking bad thoughts perhaps she would start to fly.

She thought of something nasty – chopping worms in half.

Nothing happened.

Kicking dogs. Putting slugs in people's school dinners.

Nothing happened.

Bushy Beard was nearly there. Quick – something really nasty.

Knocking old ladies to the ground and stealing their money.

Yes! She felt her feet lift off the ground a couple of centimetres. If only she could think of something worse.

'Got you!' Bushy Beard grabbed Rosie by the shoulders and shook her. 'You're a little thief and I'm taking you to the police.'

The rest of the postmen were there now and they formed a circle round her, staring down at her and nodding their heads at what Bushy Beard was saying.

He shook her hard again and his fingers dug into her shoulders spitefully.

'I'm going to make you sorry for this, milady. Trying to make a fool of me. Causing a ruckus. You're going to get what's coming to you.'

Bushy Beard's chest puffed out, his big bushy beard wagged up and down and his little eyes glared at her.

'You big bully,' Rosie thought, glaring back at him. 'I'd like to set fire to your silly whiskers and watch them sizzle and frizzle.'

There was a jerking movement and she rose a few centimetres into the air.

Bushy Beard gripped her shoulders tighter but his eyes opened wide in shock.

'What was that? What are you doing?' he gulped.

'Oh yes,' Rosie thought. 'Just like a bully – big and boasting when you think you can get your own way, but just a little scaredy-cat underneath. Huh! If I had a gun you'd soon change your tune.'

That did it. The thought flashed across her brain, hot and angry, and she felt an enormous power build up inside her.

Bushy Beard was struggling to hold her down but his eyes were filled with fear. Slowly, she raised her hand and pointed her fingers at him like a gun. He squealed in fright and let go of her shoulders.

Whooosh! She shot up into the air like a rocket and came to a stop level with the roof of the shop.

Below her the postmen were staring up in terror. They stood there for a second and then bolted in all directions like scared rabbits.

Rosie laughed and was surprised to hear how old and cackly her voice sounded. Of course, it sounded different because *she* was different. She was a Djinn.

She wasn't sure what it was going to be like to be a Djinn but so far it was rather good. She was flying and it felt great. And she had frightened old Bushy Beard out of his wits and she was glad.

She cackled again and rose higher into the air.

Oh, flying was wonderful. How jealous all her friends would be. They would probably be scared of her when she showed them what she could do. What fun it would be to see the fright in their eyes as she dive-bombed them from the air.

She could scare anyone she wanted to. She was powerful and dangerous and if anyone got in her way she would show them . . .

'He-he he-he-he,' she cackled, and rose higher and higher.

Chapter Ten

Rosie flew high over the town.

Everything looked so tiny below her. The cars and houses looked smaller than toys, and people were just little black dots like ants.

'People are small and stupid,' she thought to herself. 'When you see them from up here they're almost nothing. I'm much better and cleverer than they are. Just think how silly I made Bushy Beard look. I really gave him a fright. And the others too. They thought they could catch me but I showed them. Yes, people are just like ants and I could stamp on them and squash them.'

She rose higher still and found herself flying through the clouds.

'Only special people like me can fly like this,' she thought. 'I can do anything. I could make it rain on all those stupid people who live in that silly toy-town down there. In fact, I will.'

She held out her hands in front of her and shouted, 'Rain!'

There was a low rumble of thunder around her and she dived down out of the clouds. Yes, it was raining. All those people below were getting wet because of her. Good job – it served them right.

'Stop raining,' she ordered.

At once the rain stopped falling.

'There, I've saved them from getting too wet. They ought to be grateful to me. Yes, they all ought to get down on their knees and thank me. I can do anything. I can make them wet or I can keep them dry. I could even hit them with lightning and frizzle them up like bacon.'

She laughed at the thought. What a great idea. She could send a great big zigzagging flash of lightning.

She could feel the power bubbling up inside her. If she held her hands out and hated hard enough, the lightning would flash out from the ends of her fingers and go whizzing down to earth and hit somebody.

A quiet little voice in the back of her head asked, 'Yes, Rosie, but who would it hit?'

Anybody. Anybody. It didn't matter – they were all nothings. It could be . . .

A couple of pictures flashed across her mind. The first one was of Mum standing at the front door smiling. The second one was of Dad kneeling next to the bath and laughing as Jimmy splashed water at him during bath-time.

Yes, of course, the lightning might hit them. It might even hit . . . And she got a clear picture of Mark's cheeky face. Again she saw her young brother running towards her this morning and asking for a kiss goodbye.

She seemed to see it all – even more clearly than

she had at the time: Mark's fair hair; the funny way his lip curled when he smiled; the gap between his two front teeth; the collar of his bright check shirt against his pale neck, and the red and black sweat-shirt with the words DAKOTA TRAIL written on it.

Oh no, she couldn't let lightning hit him. Or Jimmy, or Mum, or Dad. Or, she realized with a shiver, anybody. She didn't want to hurt anybody. She wasn't better or cleverer than the rest of the world – she was just Rosie. And she didn't want to be a Djinn.

Tears filled her eyes. At the same moment the sun burst from behind the clouds and its golden light danced in her tears. The light and the tears dazzled her and she could hardly see, but it felt as if she was getting lower and lower.

She brushed the tears from her eyes and looked down. Yes, she was going back to the ground. She could see the streets and the houses clearly again.

How strange it was. Usually you could only see a small part of things, but up here you could see how all the small things fitted together. You could see how each street joined another street and how they all criss-crossed to make up the whole town.

There was the park. And there, not far away, was her own road. She could even see her home. Perhaps she was going to land right in her own garden.

She swept lower and lower, almost brushing the

54

roof-tops, and then suddenly she seemed to lose power altogether and started to dive towards some gardens in the road next to hers.

She tried to control her speed by flapping her arms, but she still came in too fast and went tumbling on to the lawn. She rolled over and over, then stopped and sat up. It had been a rough landing but she hadn't broken anything.

She got up and was beginning to brush herself down when there was a terrible growling noise behind her.

Chapter Eleven

Rosie looked round and saw a huge Alsatian dog leap out of a kennel and charge across the lawn towards her. She wanted to run but her feet wouldn't move, and she just stood there as the dog raced closer and closer.

She saw the Alsatian spring into the air. She saw it open its jaws and she saw its sharp teeth aiming at her face.

Then, at the last moment, the Alsatian jerked back and fell to the ground so suddenly that she thought it must have been shot. Then she heard a clink as the dog rolled over on to its feet again and she saw that it was on a long chain which led back to the kennel.

Rosie just had time to think how those teeth would have slashed through her face if the chain had been any longer, when the dog jumped once more. Again the chain pulled it down but this time she felt a strange anger build up inside her and, as the Alsatian got to its feet, she pointed her finger and stared hard at it.

The dog yelped as if she had hit it.

It turned round and slunk back to its kennel with its ears flat and its tail between its legs. It crept into the kennel and then peeped out at her. She took a step nearer and the poor creature whined in fright and cowered further back into the kennel.

Part of her was pleased that she had scared the dog, but another part of her felt sorry for him and another part was worried by how powerful she was. To be able to scare a fierce guard-dog like that must mean that the Djinn side of her was getting stronger. And midnight was coming closer every minute.

She had to get that parcel back to the real Djinn before it was too late.

Rosie ran to the end of the garden, through the back gate, and out into the alley that led down to the street. In a couple of minutes she was back at her own house. She got her key out and opened the front door.

It was so lovely to stand in the hall and see all the old familiar things. Jimmy's teddy bear was lying at the bottom of the stairs and she picked it up and hugged it.

Oh, if only Jimmy and the rest of them were here.

How she would love to be able to take Mark's hand and go for a walk with him, telling him the kind of stories that he loved to hear. How wonderful it would be to kiss Mum and smell her perfume, or to jump into Dad's arms and let him whirl her round.

But she couldn't do any of those things. The house was empty. Quiet, cold and empty. She was alone.

She walked to the front door to shut it and suddenly remembered the Finders. She had been through so many amazing adventures since she had last spoken to them outside the sorting office that she had forgotten all about them.

Of course she wasn't alone. They were with her, even if she couldn't see them. And, in a way, they were more important than her own family at the moment because they could help her against the Djinn.

'Mr Ikbal, Sidri,' she said. 'Are you in here or still outside?'

There was silence in the house. She turned to the front garden and called more loudly, 'Mr Ikbal, Sidri – come in.'

Still there was silence.

'Mr Ikbal! Sidri!' she yelled at the top of her voice.

No reply. Just the far-off barking of a dog.

She waited for a full minute, hoping to hear the gruff voice of Mr Ikbal or Sidri's babyish squeak, but nothing happened.

She closed the door and the truth hit her. Somewhere in all the excitement they had lost track of her. She was alone. Tears began to fill her eyes.

She took her rucksack off and pulled out the parcel. It tingled in her hand and she quickly put it down on the stairs. She hated the parcel and she hated the Djinn Star. Minute by minute it was turning her into something horrible. And there was no one to help her and she didn't know what to do.

The hot tears trickled from her eyes and began

to stream down her face, and she ran into the front room and threw herself on to the sofa. Her mind burned with all the strange things that were happening to her and she couldn't think straight. She was scared and alone. She didn't even feel like herself any more. And above all she was very, very tired.

She knew she shouldn't sleep. There wasn't much time left. She didn't have time for sleep. But she was so very, very tired . . .

She was in a dark cave and there were drums pounding. Could it be cannibals? Boom, boom, boom. Where were they? Boom, boom.

Rosie woke up with a start.

No drums. It was just a dream.

She blinked. The room was dark. It was nearly

night outside – she must have been asleep for ages.

Knock, knock, knock.

It wasn't drums she had heard. Someone was knocking at the front door.

Her legs felt a bit weak as she got up from the sofa and they wobbled slightly as she walked across the room. She switched on the light and went into the hall.

Knock, knock, knock.

'I'm coming,' she said, and reached up and opened the front door.

It swung open and Rosie gasped in shock.

Two horrible monsters were standing on the doorstep.

Chapter Twelve

Rosie just had time to see horns, glowing red eyes, and long pointed jaws before she slammed the door shut. She double-locked it quickly, then leaned against it to stop the monsters from forcing their way in.

The door shook as the knocker banged again.

She leaned harder against the door, then screamed as she felt the letter-box flap open and press into her back. A big hand like an ape's came

through and tried to grab her hand.

She fell forward on to her knees, scrambled to her feet again and dashed towards the stairs. She would run upstairs, open one of the windows and scream for help. Perhaps someone would rescue her before the monsters managed to smash through the door and trap her.

She was half-way up the stairs when a gruff voice called, 'Rosie.'

Mr Ikbal.

She was safe. The Finders had come back just in time.

'Where are you?' she called.

'Outside.'

'What about the monsters?'

She heard Sidri giggle, then the letter-box opened and his voice squeaked through. 'There aren't monsters. We couldn't find you anywhere, Wosie. Where did you go?'

Rosie started down the stairs. No monsters? Had she imagined them? So many strange things were happening to her – perhaps she had started to see things that weren't there. Or perhaps they had run away when the Finders had arrived.

Oh, she was so glad they had found her. They would know what to do next.

She unlocked the door and opened it.

This time the first thing she saw were huge frogs' feet and hairy apes' bodies. The monsters were still there. And this time she wasn't quick enough to get the door closed before they stepped into the house.

In terror, she spun round and ran into the front room. She bumped into the sofa, fell over, got up and then crashed against the far wall.

She was trapped. The dim shapes of the monsters were filling the doorway. There was no way out.

Her legs gave way under her and she slid to the floor.

'Go away,' she tried to shout, but the words only came out in a feeble whisper.

The two dark figures moved towards her across the room with their red eyes glowing in the darkness. She huddled closer to the wall and hid her face with her hands.

The monsters came nearer. Their breath sounded in her ears.

Then a small, soft furry hand started to stroke her hands.

'Wosie, why don't you say hello? It's me and Mr Ikbal.'

She kept her face hidden. Could these terrible monsters really be Sidri and Mr Ikbal?

'I understand what has happened,' Mr Ikbal said. 'You can see us, can't you, Rosie?'

She nodded.

'And if I'm not mistaken, you can see something horrible – something that frightens you.'

She nodded again.

Mr Ikbal sighed. Then she felt a large furry paw begin to stroke her hands.

'Try not to be afraid, my dear. I think I can

guess what all this is about. You've been flying, haven't you?'

'I had to. The postmen caught me and it was the only way to get away,' Rosie blurted out, taking her hands away from her face but putting them back quickly when she saw the dark figures so close to her.

'I'm sure you had a good reason,' Mr Ikbal said, 'but, just as I warned you, it has made you more like a Djinn. That's why you can see us now.'

'But why are you so . . . so . . .' Rosie stopped, not knowing quite how to say it. 'You said you were angels, but you look like . . . like devils.'

There was a squeaky gasp from Sidri and he pulled his hand away from hers, but Mr Ikbal just chuckled gruffly and went on stroking her.

'Well, my dear, that's because it's the evil side of you that is seeing us.'

'I don't understand,' Rosie said, taking her hands away from her face but keeping her eyes squeezed shut.

'Well,' Mr Ikbal said, 'how you see things depends on who you are and what is happening to you. If you were thirsty in the middle of the desert, you would be very happy if it started to rain. But if you lived next to a river that was nearly flooding you would be very unhappy if it started to rain. The rain is the same, but how you see it is different. In the same way, because Djinn hate angels they see us as horrible monsters. We are what we are – how you see us depends on you.'

Rosie suddenly felt very sad. Mr Ikbal's gruff voice was so kind and gentle, and while she hadn't been able to see them the Finders had seemed like friends. It was terrible that she had become so much of a Djinn that even little Sidri with his baby voice looked like a monster to her.

Mr Ikbal was right: it had all begun while she was flying – she could remember how, when she was high in the sky, she had hated the whole world and all the people in it. That's what it must be like to be a Djinn – you could do all sorts of interesting things but you would be filled with hatred all the time.

'Oh, Mr Ikbal,' she said, 'I don't want to become a Djinn. I liked it when I was flying, but I kept having these scary feelings. I felt as if I didn't care about anyone and that I could hurt people. It was horrible.'

'There, there, my dear,' he said, taking her hand and squeezing softly. 'It's a good sign that you didn't like it. Really evil people stop caring about anybody else. You're not like that, so there's hope yet. What we must do is get that Djinn Star back to the Djinn as soon as possible. First of all, though, we ought to eat something to keep our strength up – we're going to need it. Do you think you can be brave enough to open your eyes and show us what we can eat?'

Rosie was still rather scared at having to look at them, so the Finders stayed in the front room while she went out into the kitchen.

What could she give them to eat? Rosie looked in the fridge, then in all the cupboards, but she couldn't decide what to put on the table.

'Excuse me,' she called. 'I'm not exactly sure what mons – what angels like to eat.'

'Well, I rather like cheese and pickle, if you have any,' Mr Ikbal replied. 'But since this is Sidri's first trip and he isn't used to food on this side, he ought to have something simple. Perhaps he would like some of those breakfast things all you young human beings seem to enjoy.'

Rosie cut some bread and put it on the table with a big chunk of cheese and a jar of pickles. Then she got out the flakes and raisins for Sidri.

'It's ready,' she called.

She heard Mr Ikbal and Sidri come along the hall and pretended to be doing something at the sink so that she wouldn't have to look at them. The chairs scraped on the floor as they sat down, then there was a long silence. She still didn't look round.

'Isn't Wosie going to eat too?' Sidri finally whispered.

'I'm not very hungry, thank you,' she said quickly.

'You really ought to eat, my dear,' Mr Ikbal said. 'You'll need strength more than any of us. Come and sit with us. Remember, whatever we look like to you, we are your friends and there's nothing to be scared of.'

His voice was so kind and friendly that Rosie felt it would be rude to refuse. Looking at her feet all the time, she walked over to the table and sat down.

'Can we start now?' Sidri asked.

'I think we can,' Mr Ikbal said. 'Now, I believe you pour the raisins and flakes into the bowl and add milk. Is that right, Rosie?'

'Yes,' she said. She still didn't dare to look up but she thought she ought to make things easier by talking a bit more. 'Sometimes my brother Mark messes around and puts the milk in first. He loves flakes and raisins and he has them every morning, except sometimes when he has crispies and raisins.'

'Mmm,' Sidri said as he scrunched the flakes. 'Angels love flakes and raisins too.'

Rosie cut only a thin slice of bread and a small chunk of cheese, but as soon as she started eating she realized how hungry she was. After all, she hadn't eaten since breakfast this morning and she had had the most amazing day, full of strange adventures. And almost the strangest thing of all was to be sitting here cutting some more bread while opposite her were . . .

Were what? She took a deep breath and looked.

Sidri was just eating the last spoonful of cereal and she watched it disappear into a mouth that looked rather like a small crocodile's. A big pink tongue came out and licked the last drop of milk from the spoon and then a furry paw reached up and wiped the long snout full of sharp teeth. Then the two red eyes looked directly at her. They blinked and crinkled up into a smile.

'Can I have some more, Wosie? It's lovely.'

'Of course you can.'

She passed the jar of raisins and the box of flakes just as if she was passing them to Mark. Here she was eating with angels who looked like monsters and it was beginning to seem the most ordinary thing in the world.

In no time at all they were eating and chatting away like old friends. She told them what had happened after she ran out of the sorting office, and they told her about how hard it had been to follow her trail to her house.

'Well,' said Mr Ikbal at last, 'we ought to get going – we've all had plenty to eat. In fact, by the look of your tummy, Sidri, you've had more than enough.'

'I can still eat some more raisins – they're lovely.'

'Oh no you can't, my lad. You'll burst if you eat any more. Besides, time's getting short. I wanted Rosie to hand back the parcel just before midnight but she's getting more like a Djinn every minute so I think she'll have to do it as soon as possible. Of course, that will make the whole thing much more dangerous.'

'Oh dear,' said Rosie, suddenly feeling very weak.

'Don't worry,' Mr Ikbal said. 'It's not going to be easy, but I've got a plan.'

Chapter Thirteen

Rosie put on her jeans and looked at herself in the mirror. Even with her long hair clipped up tight on the top of her head she still didn't look much like a boy.

She ran into her parents' bedroom and found one of her dad's ties. She took ages to knot it properly and even when she got it right it didn't change her very much.

'It's no good, Mr Ikbal,' she said as she went down the stairs. 'I still look like a girl.'

'H'm, yes you do. Now let's see.' Mr Ikbal's eyes glowed redder than ever as he looked round the hall. 'Wait a minute – what about this?'

He reached up to the hat-stand and took down the flat cap that her dad wore when he went fishing. She put it on her head, tucked her hair up into it, and looked in the mirror. It was better – but it still wasn't right.

'I've got an idea,' she said, and ran upstairs to the boys' bedroom.

Their toys were all over the floor as usual and Rosie searched for nearly five minutes before she found what she was looking for.

It was a pretend moustache that Mark had got

out of a cracker last Christmas. He had liked it more than all his other presents and for nearly three weeks he had worn it every day, but now it was crushed up at the bottom of the toy-box.

The moustache was only made from thin strands of black plastic, but when Rosie pulled and straightened it back to its proper shape it looked like the real thing.

She pressed it hard up against her top lip and

was pleased to find that the sticky bit still gripped. She waggled her head around but the moustache stuck fast.

Good. Now to see what the Finders thought.

'Oh, my word, that looks almost real,' Mr Ikbal

said when he saw her, while Sidri sat down on the floor in surprise and laughed and laughed.

'Can I have a go, Wosie?' he said when he got his breath back.

'Not now, Sidri,' Mr Ikbal said. 'Rosie will let you try it later, but at the moment we've got to get moving or we'll be too late.'

The night was chilly and a full moon was rising over the top of the shed as Rosie pulled her bike out and wheeled it along the side path towards the road. Mr Ikbal and Sidri were hovering about two metres above the front gate, ready to go.

'Why don't I fly too?' Rosie asked. 'It would be much quicker.'

'Yes, it would be quicker,' Mr Ikbal agreed, 'but by the time we got there you would have become a full Djinn and it would be too late to save you. Remember that every time you use any of your powers – like flying – you become more like a Djinn. That's why you mustn't use any magic like curses or spells to help you get that Djinn Star back to its owner.'

'Oh, Mr Ikbal,' she said, feeling her tummy sink at the thought of what she had to do, 'can I really make him think I'm a man with this disguise?'

'To be honest, I just don't know,' he said. 'We'll have to hope that even if he notices how small you are he won't recognize you. I'm pretty sure his greediness will make him grab the parcel before he even bothers to take a good look at you.'

'How do you know he's greedy?' Rosie asked.

'All Djinn are greedy,' Sidri said quickly. 'We learned that in Djinn-finding lessons.'

'Quite right, lad – well remembered,' Mr Ikbal said, patting his young helper on the head. 'All evil things are greedy – always wanting more of everything: more attention, more power, more of this and more of that. They puff themselves up and think they can take anything they want, as if nobody else counts. You humans are a bit like that too – you tend to forget that you are only a tiny, tiny part of the whole of Creation.'

Mr Ikbal said this in a very kind voice but Rosie blushed, as the words went straight to her heart.

When she had been flying she had seen how all the houses and streets fitted together to make the whole town. It had made her realize that she was only one of thousands and thousands of people in the town and that she wasn't nearly as special and important as she sometimes felt.

And now, listening to Mr Ikbal, she realized that he could probably see not just the town but the whole world from very far away and that he understood how it fitted in with the rest of the universe.

She looked up at him, hovering in the air, and she knew he was wiser than anyone she had ever met. His crocodiley mouth seemed to smile at her, and one of the red eyes winked as if he knew what she was thinking. He might still look like a monster to her but she was sure that he really was an angel.

'Now then, Rosie,' he asked, 'where does that old Djinn live?'

Rosie took the parcel from the carrier on her bike and read out the name of the village.

'Boglin. It's about four miles away, near the sea. Oh, look at his name – Robin Goodfellow. It makes him sound quite friendly.'

'Not at all,' Mr Ikbal said. 'It's not his real name, of course, but he's chosen a name that people used for the Devil in the old days. And have you noticed that if you change the letters round, BOGLIN also spells GOBLIN. No wonder he chose to live there.'

'Oh, and look at the name of the house,' Rosie gasped, as a shiver ran up the back of her neck. 'It's called Gallows Tree Cottage.'

'It sounds a bit scary, sir,' said Sidri.

'Yes, it does,' admitted Mr Ikbal, 'but, as you've been told many times, Djinn are always scary. Rule One for Finders is: be on your guard and keep your wits about you all the time. Come on, no point in worrying about what might or might not happen. It's best to get on and get it over with.'

Chapter Fourteen

The journey out of town was all downhill and
Rosie sped along without having to pedal. The
wheels of the bike whizzed round and the steady
scrunch and hum of her tyres were the only noises
on the quiet roads.

It was fully dark now and everybody was indoors.
What a shock they would have if they looked out of
their windows and saw a girl, dressed up as a man,
cycling past, with two monsters flying along on
either side of her.

But, of course, they wouldn't be able to see the
Finders. It was only because she was turning into a
Djinn that Rosie was able to see them.

An owl hooted in the darkness. She looked up
and saw the black shape of a bird fly in front of the
big, golden moon. Was that the owl? It looked
more like the crow that had followed her everywhere since she had got the Djinn Star.

And now that she had been reminded of the
crow she also started to notice how many cats there
were everywhere. Of course, cats loved to be out at
night, but surely there weren't usually as many as
this?

Wherever she looked she could see them – sitting

on walls, gliding like shadows along the pavement or perching on branches of trees. And as she rode past they all turned their heads and stared at her.

Cats. Crows. Djinn. Magic. It was all so scary.

As they neared the edge of the town there were fewer and fewer houses until, finally, all the lights stopped and they were out into the countryside.

They crossed the bridge over the river and Rosie noticed the moon shining big and full on the water. The reflection shimmered and shook on the river stream and it was so beautiful that she just had to stop.

Mr Ikbal and Sidri went flying on ahead, but she just had to look up at the moon. It was so huge and so close that it seemed to be sitting on the very top of the pine trees on the hill. The brightness dazzled her and she wanted to look away, but her eyes felt as if they were locked on to the pale gold light streaming out of the sky.

Even as she stared at it, the moon seemed to glow brighter and the gold became more and more silvery, and she started to notice the dark patches that people always said looked like a face.

And it was true, it did.

She had never seen it so clearly before – but those two dark patches looked like eyes, and that line was the nose and that other patch below was the mouth.

It was so much like a face that she began to giggle and the mouth shape on the moon seemed to turn up at the sides as if it was starting to laugh with her. She giggled even more and suddenly the whole face crinkled up into a big welcoming smile.

Rosie found herself smiling back and she wanted to reach out and grab the moon and hug it close like a cuddly toy. It was so beautiful and funny and friendly that she wanted to fly up to it and live there for ever. How happy she would be. And all she had to do was let go and fly.

Never mind all that silly nonsense about not being supposed to fly. It didn't matter. And – oh look – the big smiling mouth of the moon was opening and he was starting to sing, and his soft, silky voice was throbbing in her ears:

I'm a big fat moon
That shines like a spoon
I'm as round as a balloon
So listen to my tune

Yes, listen to my tune
Cos you've got the rune
So come and join us soon.

Round and round the tune went – slowly at first, but getting faster and faster, until all she could hear was 'Moon, Spoon, Balloon, Tune, Rune, Soon.'

Then the whole moon began to spin. Faster and faster it turned until there was just a silvery blur in front of her and she wanted to fly, fly, fly.

'Rosie! Rosie!' A gruff voice came floating through the singing and spinning.

And now a high voice came floating through the singing and spinning. 'Wosie! Wosie!'

It was Mr Ikbal and Sidri. Where were they? In the moon? She would fly to the moon and see them. Yes, that's what she would do.

But her legs felt so heavy. She wanted to fly but her feet were stuck and she felt as if she was swimming in the sea and her feet had got caught in the jaws of a giant clam.

Moon, Spoon, Balloon, Tune, Rune, Soon.

Rosie. Wosie. Don't!

She snapped out of the dream, and the singing and the spinning stopped.

She found herself hovering above the bridge with Mr Ikbal and Sidri hanging on to her feet. They were the ones who had stopped her flying. A flash of fury swept through her. How dare they? She would teach them a lesson by sending a bolt of lightning to frizzle them up.

Then, as she raised her hands, she realized they were her friends and they were trying to help her. She felt herself relax and she let them pull her back down to the bridge.

'Oh, Mr Ikbal – what happened to me?' she asked in a trembling voice.

'Moon madness, my dear. The moon has great power. It is powerful enough to make the seas and oceans move backwards and forwards in tides and, in the same way, it has a very strong attraction for Djinn. It makes them want to fly and they often do their magic at night by its light.'

'And what's a rune?' she asked. 'I kept hearing this song and it mentioned "rune".'

'It's ancient writing that was often used in magic spells. There's a very strong rune written on the Djinn Star and that's what has been taking you over and turning you into a Djinn.'

'Oh, Mr Ikbal, perhaps it's too late. Perhaps I'm already a Djinn and I won't ever be able to be me again.'

'Stuff and nonsense, my dear. Even an apprentice like young Sidri can see that there's plenty of good left in you yet – isn't that true, lad?'

Sidri turned his glowing red eyes towards her

and started to nod his head, but his big crocodiley jaws slowly opened wide and the nodding stopped. His eyes grew larger and larger and his head began to shake slowly.

'Mr Ikbal,' he gasped. 'I can't. I can't see the goodness – it's gone.'

Mr Ikbal's head jerked round to her and his eyes glowed a fierce red as they peered at her.

'Oh dear, oh dear,' he murmured. 'That tricky old moon has made matters worse. I'm afraid there's little time left. How much further is it to Boglin?'

'About a mile,' Rosie said, feeling her mouth go dry with fright.

'Sidri is not right – I can still see a glow of goodness from within you, but it's getting dangerously faint. Now, get on that bike and ride for all you're worth. And for goodness' sake don't look at the moon, and try to keep your mind on good things. Quick, quick – before it's too late!'

Chapter Fifteen

A mist was rising from the fields and the night air was growing chilly. Rosie pumped up and down on the pedals, pushing the bike as hard as she could. Her breath came out in clouds of steam and the cold wind made her eyes water, so she had to keep wiping the tears away in order to keep the bike on a steady course.

Strange pictures kept flashing across her brain – coming before she could stop them and going almost before she could see what they were: a beach where the waves turned into blood; a street with all the houses on fire . . .

The pictures were cruel and horrible but she could feel that part of her was excited by them. And at the back of her mind she could still hear that song whispering to her, telling her to look up at the moon.

She tried to drive the pictures and the song away by thinking of other songs. The only tune that seemed to work was 'Happy Birthday', so, as the road began to slope up towards Boglin, she chanted out loud:

> *Happy Birthday to you,*
> *Happy Birthday to you.*

When she got to the name she couldn't think of anybody, so she sang:

Happy Birthday, dear Sidri,
Happy Birthday to you.

There was a little laugh from above her, but she didn't dare look up in case she caught a glimpse of the moon.

'It's not my birthday,' Sidri said, 'not for another ninety-nine years.'

'Ninety-nine years?' Rosie gasped.

'That's right,' said Mr Ikbal. 'We only celebrate our birthdays every one hundred years, by your time. Sidri has just had his first birthday and his second will be in ninety-nine years' time.'

'How old are you, Mr Ikbal?' Rosie asked, hoping it wasn't a rude question.

'Oh, me, I've been around a very long time – longer than you could possibly imagine.'

She was going to ask him how long that was, but the moon song started up again in her mind, so she quickly began to sing 'Happy Birthday'. This time she said 'Dear Jimmy', the next time it was 'Dear Mark' and then 'Dear Mum' and finally 'Dear Dad'.

As she sang each of the names she tried to picture their faces as clearly as she could, and the thoughts made her feel stronger. She couldn't let herself become a Djinn. She had to fight and fight to make sure that she would be able to go home to her family and be the Rosie she had always been.

'Ssh, I think you'd better stop singing now,' Mr Ikbal said.

When she looked up, Rosie saw why. There was a sign which said BOGLIN in big black letters and down the road were the houses that made up the little village. Rosie shivered. Somewhere, in one of those houses, perhaps the Djinn was waiting for her.

They went slowly along the main street, peering at the names on the garden gates: 'Hillside Cottage', 'Sea View', 'Cliff Cottage', 'Four Winds' – there were all kinds of names, but no 'Gallows Tree Cottage'.

When they got to the end of the street they were almost at the edge of the cliff and the sea sparkled below them. Even the glittery reflection of the moon on the waves seemed to call to Rosie, so she turned away quickly and looked back at the village.

'I think we'll have to go back and ask someone,' she said.

'Good idea,' said Sidri, giving her an encouraging pat on her shoulder.

There was nobody on the streets. Everybody was probably sitting, warm and comfortable, in front of their fires. Rosie wheeled her bike, daring herself to knock at one of the houses, but it wasn't until the very last one that she plucked up the courage.

She left her bike against the fence, opened the gate and went up the path. Taking a deep breath, she pulled the knocker back and banged loudly. The door opened almost at once, as if the man had been waiting for someone to knock.

'Yes?' he said.

'I'm sorry to disturb you but can you tell me where Gallows Tree Cottage is?'

The man cupped his hand to his ear and said, 'I'm sorry, young man, can you speak up. I'm a little deaf.'

Rosie had completely forgotten that she was disguised, so when she repeated the question she tried to make her voice sound as deep as she could.

Again, the man cupped his hand to his ear and said, 'Sorry?'

Rosie pulled the parcel from her pocket and pointed to the address.

The man bent down until his face was almost touching the parcel. His thick glasses made his eyes seem very large as he peered at the writing.

'Robin Goodfellow – never heard of him. Doesn't live here,' he said, but then he caught sight of the address. 'Oh, Gallows Tree Cottage – that's where Miss Kittie and Miss Rooke live. He must be staying with them, lucky chap. They are two of the nicest ladies who have ever walked this earth. They've only lived here for a couple of months, but they've made friends with everybody. They bake the most delicious cakes too, and give them to all the villagers.'

He pointed his finger past Rosie.

'You'll find their house over there. You take that lane opposite, go past the church, then turn left at the end. You can't miss it.'

She started to say 'Thank you', but the man

stepped back into the house and closed the door before she could finish. She walked back down the path, with Mr Ikbal and Sidri hovering on either side of her.

'Perhaps there's been a mistake,' she said when they got back to the road. 'Surely a Djinn wouldn't choose to live with ladies like Miss Kittie and Miss Rooke. They sound really nice.'

'Don't jump to conclusions about them, my dear,' Mr Ikbal said. 'Human beings are the cleverest animals in the world when it comes to hiding the truth about themselves.'

Rosie got hold of her bike and they crossed the road in the direction of the church.

'Besides,' Mr Ikbal continued, 'the man said the ladies have only been here for a short time. Often the people who seem kind and friendly at first turn out to be quite different later. And I'd like to know what they put in those cakes that they're so anxious to give to people. It might be some kind of magic herb that stops people from seeing the truth. And another thing – those names. I told you that Djinn often have crows and cats near them – well, kittie is a pet name for a cat and a rook is a kind of crow.'

A shiver ran up and down Rosie's back.

'Oh, Mr Ikbal, perhaps they know I'm coming.'

'Perhaps they do, my dear, but it's too late to change our plan now. You have to get that parcel back to the Djinn as soon as possible. You must be very brave and hope that Mr Robin Goodfellow, as he likes to call himself, doesn't see through your disguise. That old man you just spoke to didn't realize you were a girl.'

As they started up the lane Rosie tried to comfort herself that the old man had been fooled by her disguise, but she couldn't help feeling that it wouldn't be so easy to trick the people at Gallows Tree Cottage.

After all, that old man at the house couldn't hear or see very well, but she would never forget the way the pale-blue eyes of the Djinn had stared at her so fiercely when he had given her the parcel. They had seemed to look right through her. Surely eyes like that would see through her silly disguise in a moment?

Suddenly she felt very weak and afraid.

Chapter Sixteen

Rosie was glad that she was wheeling her bike and could hold on tight to the handlebars to stop her hands from shaking.

Mr Ikbal must have sensed how scared she was because his voice whispered in her ear, 'Courage, my dear. Think of the people you love and make up your mind that you will do all you can to stop yourself becoming a Djinn.'

She turned and smiled at him to show that she would try as hard as she could, and at that moment Sidri's high voice whispered in her other ear.

'I'm glad you're here, Wosie,' the young angel said. 'I'm not very, very scared but, see, it's my first mission and I might be a bit scared, but it's all right because you're here and you're brave.'

Rosie turned and smiled at him, hoping that she looked braver than she felt. Sidri hovered lower and stroked her cheek with his furry paw.

At that moment the clock in the church tower chimed loudly above them. Sidri jumped in alarm and flew up to hold on to Mr Ikbal's arm.

The noise had startled Rosie too, but when she looked up and saw that the clock showed 11.15, she realized that there wasn't time to waste in being scared. In another forty-five minutes it would be midnight and she would be a Djinn.

She pushed the bike faster and they soon came to the place where the lane turned to the left. About fifty metres away she could see the shape of a house.

'Gallows Tree Cottage,' Mr Ikbal said. 'Yes, I can feel the presence of the Djinn even from here. Now, Rosie, you must go on alone, otherwise he might sense that there are Finders around and realize what is happening. When you get to the garden gate leave your bike outside, facing this direction, because the moment you hand that parcel to the Djinn you must get away from him as quickly as you can.'

'Why?' Rosie asked. 'I thought everything would be over as soon as I gave the Djinn Star back to him.'

'Unfortunately not,' Mr Ikbal said. 'You see, the only time Finders can arrest Djinn and transport them back to the other side is at midnight. So, until that old church clock strikes twelve he will be able to use all his powers to frighten you into taking the Star back.'

Rosie could feel tears of fear begin to rise in her eyes, but she blinked them away before they could roll down her cheeks. Crying wouldn't help.

'Naturally, Sidri and I will do all we can to protect and help you,' Mr Ikbal said, giving her shoulder an encouraging squeeze, 'but the safest thing will be for you to get on that bike and ride as fast as you can. With any luck you'll be so far away that he won't even find you before his time expires. Then at the Witching Hour we'll arrest him and take him back to the other side, where he won't be able to hurt you. Now, off you go, and remember, you have all the powers of good at your back – no matter how small and scared you might feel. Come, Sidri, we must hide and wait.'

Mr Ikbal took his young apprentice's hand and they both shot off through the air and disappeared into the darkness beyond the church.

Rosie wished she could go with them.

For a moment she almost let her feet leave the ground so that she could fly after them. No. If she used her powers just once more, she would be lost for ever.

She turned and slowly wheeled the bike towards the house.

Unlike the other houses in Boglin, there was no light in any of the windows and Rosie shivered as she got nearer. When she reached the garden gate she carefully turned her bike round and leaned it up against the fence so she could grab it and race away as soon as she came out.

Quietly she opened the gate and started up the path. Her heart was beating fast and she wanted to run away, but she forced her feet to keep moving in the same direction – closer and closer to the house. Was someone watching her from behind those dark windows or was the house as empty as it seemed?

She reached the porch steps and climbed them.

One, two, three. And now, there was the door, just
in front of her.

Was there a knocker? No.

An old-fashioned bell-pull hung to the right of
the door. She reached up and pulled it. Somewhere
deep inside the house the bell tinkled.

She felt in her pocket and her hand closed round
the parcel.

A light came on in the hall and shone through
the coloured glass at the top of the door. She drew
the parcel out of her pocket and held it behind her
back. She took a deep breath as she heard footsteps
coming down the hall.

She knew what she had to do: as soon as the
Djinn opened the door she would hold out the
parcel and hope that he would take it before he

realized who she was.

There was a rattling of locks, then the door started to open. Rosie tensed, with the parcel behind her back. But, as the door swung wider, her heart sank.

Two ladies were standing there.

The Djinn was nowhere in sight. She wouldn't be able to give him the parcel and run.

And before she could think what to do, the two ladies got hold of her shoulders and pulled her into the house.

Chapter Seventeen

The door closed behind her and Rosie looked up in fear at the two ladies.

The first one was rather tubby and, although she was old, she was dressed just like a doll. She wore a frilly pink and white dress and her hair was curled into ringlets. There was heavy pink make-up on her cheeks and waves of sweet perfume rolled off her as she bent down towards Rosie.

'Welcome, welcome, welcome,' she said in a high-pitched voice, and she smiled a huge smile that showed brown-stained teeth behind her bright-red lips. 'My name's Miss Kittie and this is my friend Miss Rooke. Say hello to our itsy-bitsy visitor, Rooksie.'

'Hello,' said Miss Rooke, slapping Rosie rather hard on the back.

She had short spiky hair and was wearing a baggy old sweater, dirty corduroy trousers and heavy shoes. Her weather-beaten face had no trace of make-up and her hands were covered in dry mud, as if she had been digging in the garden all day.

'A guestie-westie,' giggled Miss Kittie, holding the skirt of her dress out and twirling round like a young girl at a party. 'I bet you've come to see Mr Goodfellow, haven't you?'

Rosie nodded.

'I knew it!' squealed Miss Kittie, spinning faster and faster. 'I've won my betsie-wetsie.'

'Oh, do stop that dancing,' snapped Miss Rooke. 'You're making me feel dizzy. Anyway, nobody took your bet, so you haven't won anything.'

'Sorry, Rooksie,' panted Miss Kittie as she stopped twirling. Suddenly she pointed at the parcel in Rosie's hand. 'Oh look – a present for Mr Goodfellow. He will be pleased – he loves pressie-wessies, doesn't he, Rooksie? Isn't it kind of the nice young gentleman?'

Rosie felt a blush creep up her neck and into her cheeks. Were these two strange old ladies laughing at her, or had they really been fooled by her disguise?

She reached up and touched her moustache. Yes, it was still there. Perhaps she did look like a man. And yet she couldn't help feeling that there were hidden messages in the glances that the two ladies were giving each other.

'Is Mr Goodfellow in?' she asked, making her voice as deep as possible.

'Oh yes, he's here, don't worry,' Miss Rooke said, and Rosie was aware of how very deep and growly her voice was. Did she always talk like that or was she making fun of Rosie's voice? 'Come along, you can wait for him in the study.'

'That's right, Rooksie,' said Miss Kittie, 'you

take the young man to the study-wudy and I'll pop
to the kitchen to get something nice to eat and
drink. Hip, hip, hooray.'

Miss Kittie skipped away into the kitchen and
Miss Rooke took hold of Rosie's shoulder and
guided her along the hall. The study was at the
very end of the hall and the heavy door creaked as
Miss Rooke pushed it open. Rosie felt a wave of
fear pass through her and she had a sudden urge to
run away. She sensed that something terrible lay in
wait for her in that room. But Miss Rooke's
fingers pressed hard into her shoulder and she had
no choice but to go inside.

There was only one small lamp on the desk and
its dim light cast deep shadows all around, but
Rosie could see that nearly everything in the room
was of a dark-brown colour. The walls were covered
with dark wood panelling, the long curtains were
dark-brown velvet, the chairs were covered in dark
leather and even the books on the bookshelf were
brown.

Rosie had a horrible feeling that from the dark
shadows of the room eyes were looking at her, and
when she peered closer she saw it was true.

Dead, glassy eyes stared at her from the walls,
where heads of lions and tigers, deer and rhino
hung in rows. From the tops of every bookcase and
sideboard she could see the dim shapes of the
stuffed bodies of birds and small animals, and in
the corner near the fireplace stood a wolf with its
lips curled into a snarl.

'Aren't they gorgeous?' said Miss Rooke, when she saw what Rosie was looking at. 'Mr Goodfellow killed them all himself – he's a wonderful hunter; nothing ever escapes from him.'

Rosie thought they looked horrible, but she was too scared to say anything. Luckily, at that moment Miss Kittie came in, carrying a tray.

'Drinkie-winkies and eatsie-weatsies,' Miss Kittie cried as she set the tray down next to a stuffed fox on the desk. The fox looked so real that it seemed as if it might spring to life at any moment and sink its sharp teeth into the big iced cake that had just been brought in.

From outside came the sound of the church clock chiming. Everybody froze and listened to it.

One. Two.

The two chimes echoed in the silence.

'Dong-ding, ding-dong,' Miss Kittie chanted. 'The old clockie-wockie tick-tocks away.'

'Half-past eleven already. How time flies,' Miss Rooke said, looking at Miss Kittie and winking quickly.

Suddenly Rosie knew they were playing with her. They knew who she was and why she was here. They knew that in half an hour she would become a Djinn and they were just keeping her here until it was too late for her to do anything.

The echo from the church clock faded away and Rosie started to get up.

'You're not going, surely?' said Miss Rooke, and pushed her back into the chair.

'Oh no, don't go,' said Miss Kittie. 'Not yet, my pet. Stay here, my dear. Don't part, my heart.'

'Give her something to eat, Kittie.'

'Yes, you must try some of my cakie-wakie. I baked it specially-wecially, didn't I, Rooksie?'

She plunged the knife into the cake and cut a huge slice, which she slid on to a plate and handed to Rosie.

'I'm not hungry, thank you,' said Rosie. She remembered what Mr Ikbal had said and she didn't want to eat anything that might have magic herbs in it.

'Oh eat it up. It's scrummy-wummy,' cooed Miss Kittie. 'What are you scared of?'

'Anyone would think we'd put squashed toad in

it or something,' Miss Rooke said, and then began to giggle.

'Squashed toadie-woadie,' snorted Miss Kittie, and joined in the giggling.

The giggles turned to chuckles and the chuckles turned to cackles and in a moment the two of them were holding on to each other, roaring with laughter.

Rosie looked down at her cake.

The icing looked perfectly normal and the sponge-cake looked perfectly normal and the cream in the middle looked perfectly normal. What were they laughing about?

Then she saw it.

From either side of the cream, a sticky, gooey green mess started to ooze out on to the plate. They meant it – there really *was* squashed toad in it. She quickly put the plate down on the desk and pushed it away from her.

The old ladies saw her do it and burst into even louder laughter.

'Oooh-ha-ha!' whooped Miss Rooke. '*He* doesn't like it! Oooh-ha-ha. *He* doesn't know what *he's* missing.'

With this she snatched up Rosie's slice of cake and crammed it into Miss Kittie's laughing mouth.

'Oooh, it's super-wuper,' Miss Kittie mumbled, and then exploded into another fit of giggles that sent bits of cake flying out of her mouth on to the floor.

'Oh, naughty, naughty,' screamed Miss Rooke,

and the two of them danced round and round, with tears of laughter running down their cheeks.

Suddenly there was the sound of a door slamming out in the hall and the two ladies stopped laughing at once.

'It's the master,' Miss Rooke said, and they began frantically picking up the pieces of cake that had splattered everywhere.

They had both gone very pale and they looked scared as they brushed the last crumbs under a chair.

Footsteps sounded outside, then the door slowly opened.

Chapter Eighteen

Rosie stood up as the old man came into the room.

At first glance he looked exactly the same as the first time she had seen him: white hair, red face and those pale-blue eyes. But as he walked towards her it was as if she could see right through him and that inside him was another man: a younger, stronger and more terrible man with thin yellow cheeks and pointed teeth.

She blinked and the young man had gone, leaving just the old man, hobbling slowly towards her with his walking-stick.

'Very well, ladies – you may leave us now,' he said coldly, keeping his eyes fixed on Rosie.

Miss Rooke and Miss Kittie bowed their heads and walked quickly to the door and out of the room.

Rosie was alone with the Djinn.

The old man sat on the edge of the desk and stared at her.

'So, young man,' he said, 'what can I do for you?'

Again, Rosie had a quick flash of someone else, as if the old man was hollow and that the real person was hidden inside him. But this time the person inside was less like a human being and more like a reptile, with a pointed scaly face and cold slit eyes.

'Well?' he asked again.

Rosie summoned up all her courage and said, 'I've got something for you.'

'Oh,' said the man, leaning forward on his stick. 'What is it?'

'This,' she said, holding out the parcel but trying to cover it with her hand so that he wouldn't see what it was.

'How nice,' said the old man, holding out his hand.

For one wonderful moment Rosie thought he was going to take the parcel, but he suddenly reached up and got hold of her moustache instead. The glue had stuck quite strongly and as he ripped the moustache away from her lip it felt as if he had taken some skin with it.

She gasped and stepped backwards in fright as he stood up. The old man had gone. Now it was the younger man with the yellow skin and pointed teeth who towered over her.

'Now, let us stop these silly games,' he said. 'You have the Djinn Star and you are very nearly one of us. That is why you can see me as I really am. Only human beings could be fooled by my old-man disguise. And you see this?'

He held up his walking-stick and waved it in front of Rosie's eyes. She wanted to look away but she couldn't.

The wooden stick seemed to be glowing. And now it began to grow longer and started to shine like bright metal. And then she saw it wasn't a stick at all. It was a sword. A dazzling sword with a blade as sharp as a razor and with a huge blood-red ruby set in its hilt.

'Yes, of course you can see it,' he said, as Rosie stared at the beautiful sword. 'No human being can see a sorcerer's sword. So, you might as well accept it. You are a Djinn and I am your master. Bow your head and swear obedience to me.'

His pale-blue eyes glared at her until she could feel his power taking her over. There was no point in resisting. In a short time, at midnight, she would have to give in. And there was no way of tricking him into taking the Star. He was right: she ought to accept that she was a Djinn.

The sword flashed to and fro and those pale-blue eyes bored into her until she felt weaker and weaker.

What did it matter if she bowed to him and became a Djinn? There was nothing she could do to stop it. And, anyway, who would care?

Mum and Dad would care. Jimmy would care. And Mark would care.

Oh yes, her young brother would miss her terribly. He would miss their friendly fights and the stories she told him. He would miss their breakfasts together.

And she would miss him. His floppy hair and his smiling eyes. His endless chanting and his corny jokes. And those little moments when he showed her just how much he really did care – like the kiss when she left him early this morning.

'Come along,' snapped the Djinn, moving closer. 'Bow your head and accept me.'

'No,' she managed to whisper.

'Very well,' he said, looking at his watch. 'I can wait. In twenty minutes' time you won't have a choice.'

He placed his sword on the edge of the desk and pulled a book from the bookshelf. He sat in the chair opposite her, calmly opened the book, and began to read.

There was such a deep silence in the room that Rosie seemed to be able to hear the tick of the clock from the distant church.

Tick-tock.

The seconds were racing past, turning into minutes. And how many minutes were left? Less than twenty. Less than twenty minutes of all the things she knew and loved. And then . . . a Djinn. For ever.

Something inside her stirred at this last thought and her head was suddenly filled with cruel ideas. What fun it would be to say unkind things to people and make them unhappy. How good it would be to see them cry. She could steal things. Spread rumours. Tell lies. Break things. Oh yes, she would have a great time.

Rosie looked up at the Djinn and found that he was smiling at her.

'Exactly, it will be wonderful fun,' he said, and she realized that he knew what she had been thinking.

How clever he was. Perhaps when she became a Djinn she would be able to read thoughts too.

'Of course you will,' he said, and held out a hand to her. 'Now come along, kiss my hand and swear obedience to me, and as a reward I will teach you how to read thoughts and I will give you all kinds of magic powers.'

Rosie found herself standing up, as if something was pulling her to her feet. Step by step she moved towards him. She knelt down in front of him and took hold of his hand. This was it. All she had to do was kiss his hand and call him 'Master' and all her worries would be over. She would be a Djinn.

She looked into his eyes and their snaky stare made her heart beat fast.

Oh, all the wonderful things she would be able to do – she would fly and read people's minds and do magic, and she would hate. Oh yes, how she would hate. And how she would hurt. And her strong, handsome master would tell her what to do and she would never have to think for herself again.

She closed her eyes and bent her head towards his hand. Her lips touched the cold skin and a shiver ran through her.

Far off, like a memory, she seemed to hear a voice calling 'No'. For a moment it sounded like Mark's voice. She tried to listen but suddenly the Djinn grabbed hold of her arm.

'Good,' he hissed. 'Now, say you accept me as your master and swear everlasting loyalty to me.'

The hand dug into her arm and pulled her towards him so that his face was so close to hers that all she could see was his eyes.

'Go on – say it,' he ordered.

'No!' Again that far-off voice floated in the air, but this time it sounded a little closer.

'Say I am your master. Swear obedience. Do it now.'

'No!' The voice came again and this time it was definitely closer. And it was not Mark's voice. It was the voice of Sidri calling out to her.

The Djinn jerked her arm and dug his finger-nails into her skin. 'Swear,' he shouted, and she saw his eyes begin to turn red. 'Swear.'

'No!' screamed the voice, and Rosie realized that it came from just outside the house.

Suddenly there was a crash of glass and the window exploded.

Chapter Nineteen

As glass from the window flew everywhere, Rosie looked up and saw Sidri come bursting through into the room.

'Leave her alone,' Sidri cried, hovering in the air above the desk.

The Djinn leaped to his feet, dragging Rosie up with him.

'She's mine,' he shouted. 'She has chosen me as her master. And you – you stupid young thing – you have made a big mistake. You are our enemy and we will destroy you. The two of us. Our power is stronger than yours.'

Sidri looked at her in shock. 'Wosie – is it true? Are you my enemy?'

Was she? Rosie's mind was spinning and the Djinn's fingers were digging into her arm. Whose side was she on?

Had she chosen the Djinn as her master? She couldn't remember. He was clever and powerful and he had promised to give her magic powers. And she knew from the pain in her arm that he could really hurt her if she made him angry. He was so strong and scary that perhaps it would be safer to be on his side.

She looked up at Sidri. He wasn't at all strong or scary. It was almost funny to think that at one time she had been terrified by him.

Look at him . . . with his crocodiley head and monkey body and frog's legs.

He looked rather like a little toy that had been put together with bits from other toys. Just a little mixed-up toy who was starting to look very weak and frightened.

'Oh dear,' Sidri said, his big eyes beginning to fill with tears, 'I thought you were my friend, Wosie. Mr Ikbal said I shouldn't come but I thought you were in danger and I wanted to help you. Oh dear.'

'You should have listened to your Mr Ikbal, you silly little meddling creature,' the Djinn said with a cold laugh. 'I don't often have the chance to get revenge on the Finders, so it is going to give me great pleasure to kill you.'

The Djinn let go of Rosie's arm and took a step towards Sidri. The young Finder rose a little higher in the air to keep himself out of the Djinn's reach and glanced over at Rosie.

He seemed so small and helpless and she suddenly remembered the moment outside when he had told her how scared he was. How brave it was of him to come bursting in here to try and rescue her. Perhaps he was her friend after all. She couldn't be sure.

She looked at the Djinn, then she looked at Sidri. Whose side was she on?

She looked back at the Djinn and saw that he was slowly stretching his arm out behind his back. He was reaching towards the desk to pick up the sorcerer's sword. She could see what was going to happen. In a moment his hand would grab hold of the sword and he would swing it into the air and kill Sidri.

And what would she feel? Would she be happy or sad? The words spun round and round in her brain. Happy. Sad.

She would be happy. Of course, she would. She didn't want a Finder to win, did she? Sidri was a Finder and she was a Djinn, wasn't she? Yes, she would laugh out loud and clap her hands when the sword cut through Mark.

Mark? No, not Mark. Sidri.

Her brain was whirling faster and faster. Mark. Sidri. She was getting confused. Whose side was she on?

She was a Djinn.

Mark. Sidri. Mum. Dad. Sidri. Jimmy. Mark. Rosie.

I am Rosie.

Her brain stopped spinning.

She wasn't a Djinn. Not yet. It wasn't midnight. She was still Rosie. Somehow she must still try to help Sidri. And somehow she mustn't let herself become a Djinn.

She looked at the Djinn. His back was towards her and he was staring up at Sidri, while his hand was creeping closer and closer to the sword.

Slowly, Rosie began to tiptoe forward. A

floorboard creaked and she held her breath in case the Djinn turned round, but he was too busy trying to find the sword without letting Sidri see what he was doing.

His hand was nearly there.

Rosie tiptoed forward again.

The Djinn's finger touched the end of the hilt. His other fingers curled, ready to grab hold of the sword.

Rosie darted forward and slipped the parcel into his hand.

A flash of silver light shot up the Djinn's arm and, as he turned round in shock, Rosie saw a star shape glowing in the middle of his forehead. It burned brightly, then faded away.

He looked down at his hand and saw the parcel.

'The Djinn Star!' he screamed. 'You've given me the Djinn Star. No! Take it back, take it back.'

Rosie stepped away from him and held her hands behind her back.

'No,' she said, quite calmly. 'No. I don't want to be a Djinn. And I don't want you to be my master.'

'Hooray,' cried Sidri from up near the ceiling. 'Rosie's won.'

'Oh no she hasn't,' shouted the Djinn as he whirled round and picked up the sword. He held it out and pressed it against Rosie's chest. She could feel its sharp point on the skin just above her heart. 'Take this parcel back or I'll run you through with my sword.'

'No you won't,' Sidri said, flying down towards them. 'I arrest you.'

At that moment the church clock began to strike. Everyone froze as the three chimes pealed out.

'It's only a quarter to twelve,' sneered the Djinn as the last chime faded away. 'You can't touch me until midnight, you ugly little pest.'

'Oh yes I can,' said Sidri, and he flew up close to the Djinn's face and pulled his ear. 'There – I touched your ear and now I'll touch the other one.'

And he began buzzing round and round the Djinn's head, pulling first one ear, then the other.

Rosie realized that Sidri was trying to draw the Djinn's attention away from her and she got ready to run as soon as there was a chance.

Suddenly the Djinn raised the sword and swiped

at Sidri, but the young Finder dodged aside and flew across the room. The Djinn went charging after him and as they both went one way, Rosie went the other.

She reached the broken window and dived headlong out into the garden.

She tumbled on to the ground and scrambled to her feet. She heard the Djinn roar, 'Get her!' and, as she glanced through the window, the door opened and the two old ladies rushed in and ran across the room towards her.

At the same time she saw the fox on the table turn its head and look towards the window. Rosie gasped in horror.

'Get her!' the Djinn screamed again.

And now all the animals began to move.

The wolf, the alligator, the weasel, the snake, the birds – all the dead, stuffed creatures came to life at his command and began to move towards the window.

Rosie screamed and fled away into the darkness.

Chapter Twenty

The bike. She must get to the bike.

She dashed along the back of the house and then down the side path to the front garden. As she got to the garden gate the front door of the house opened and Miss Rooke and Miss Kittie came running out, followed by the animals.

'Stop her!' screamed Miss Rooke as they darted across the porch and down the steps.

Rosie grabbed hold of the bike and pulled, but it was stuck fast.

The old ladies were running down the path towards her. Had they put a spell on the bike to stop it moving? Quick, they were at the gate.

Rosie looked down and saw that the brake handle had got caught in one of the wooden slats of the fence. She pulled on the handlebars and jerked the brake out of the fence.

Quick!

She stood on one pedal and began to scoot to get the bike moving. Miss Rooke was nearly there, reaching out to catch hold of her. Rosie gave one more scoot, then swung her other leg over the saddle, stood up, and pedalled like mad.

She felt Miss Rooke's fingers grab hold of the

back of her anorak but at that moment the bike
shot forward and Miss Rooke lost her grip, stumbled, and fell. First Miss Kittie, then all the
animals, went tumbling over her.

Rosie pumped her legs up and down on the
pedals and the bike whizzed down the lane. As she
sped round the corner towards the church she
looked back and saw the old ladies still on the
ground. But the animals were already scrambling

back to their feet and, led by the wolf, they began
to race along the lane after her.

The clock on the church tower showed 11.50.
Ten more minutes to go before midnight. Ten

more minutes before she would be safe. Ten minutes in which anything could happen.

The bike was going so fast that the wind was whistling in her ears, but she could hear other noises – the soft pad of paws, the sharp click of claws, and the panting of breath – growing louder behind her. The wolf and the other animals were getting closer. The thought of their sharp, snapping teeth gave extra strength to her legs and she pumped even harder on the pedals.

She reached the end of the lane and skidded round on to the road that led out of the village. If she could just get to the hill she might be able to go faster and leave the animals behind.

She glanced back and saw the grey shape of the wolf only a couple of metres away. He was gaining on her. His eyes were fixed on her legs and she could sense that he was getting ready to spring.

She flashed by the sign saying BOGLIN and the road began to dip.

As the bike gathered speed the wolf leaped.

His teeth slashed into her jeans, just missing her skin. The bike wobbled dangerously as the wolf tried to drag her back. Rosie twisted the handlebars to keep herself from falling and, at the same time, kicked her leg to free herself.

There was a loud rip and the wolf was left behind with just a shred of her jeans in his teeth.

And now, free of the wolf's weight, the bike sailed away down the hill, going faster and faster. She looked round and saw the animals stop in the middle of the road. They had given up the chase!

The chilly wind was making her eyes fill with water and the bike was whizzing along so fast that she could hardly see where she was going. The darkness raced towards her and her fingers longed to pull on the brakes, but she didn't dare slow down in case the animals caught up with her again.

She blinked the tears out of her eyes and peered ahead, but the thin beam of her front lamp was so feeble that she didn't see the bump in the road until the last moment. She swung the handlebars to try to steer round it but the front wheel hit the edge and bucked into the air. The rear wheel followed and the bike tipped to the side.

When the two wheels hit the road again she was completely off balance and nothing could stop her crashing off the road and into the woods.

The bike burst through a clump of ferns, then came to a jolting stop as it tipped forwards into a ditch. Rosie went flying head over heels and landed on her shoulder with such a thump that all the breath was knocked out of her body.

She lay for a moment, gasping for air, then she heard something that made her scramble to her feet. It was the howl of a wolf. And it was close.

And now she could hear the sounds of the whole pack of animals running down the hill. There was no time for her to get on to the bike and back on the road.

Branches poked at her and brambles snagged her clothes, but Rosie didn't let anything hold her back. She plunged wildly through the darkness of the woods with just one thought in her mind – if she could get deep among the trees the animals might not find her.

She ran for about thirty seconds, then tripped over the branch of a bush and fell.

The wolf howled again and this time she decided to stay still. Perhaps if she didn't make a noise the animals would race past, looking for her on the road.

She strained her ears to listen. The wolf howled again. Closer than before. It was still out on the road but level with where she was hiding. Had they found her?

There was a rustling and in the dim light of the moon she saw the ferns at the edge of the wood begin to shiver and shake. They had found her scent and were following her tracks through the trees.

There was no point in trying to outrun them – they'd catch her in a moment. The only thing to do was hide. She tiptoed quickly to the nearest big tree, reached up, grabbed hold of a branch, and pulled herself up.

The branches were easily spaced and she climbed fast until she was right in the heart of the old oak tree. She clung tightly to the trunk and held her breath as first the wolf, then the fox, then the rest of the animals came sniffing round the base of the tree.

For a moment a couple of them moved away,

trying to find her scent on the ground, but they quickly came back to the tree. Suddenly, as one, they all raised their heads and looked straight up at her.

There was a whirr of wings and the barn-owl came flying through the branches like a white ghost. Rosie turned her face to the trunk and almost fell as she felt a sharp peck on the back of her head. The owl flew away, circled, then headed back towards her.

She could see the cruel beak and the sharp claws coming closer, but this time she lashed out with her arm and hit the end of the owl's wing as it swept past. The bird rocked from side to side as some of its feathers fell out, then it flapped away and landed in a beech tree. Its big eyes glared angrily at her but it didn't look as if it was very keen on making another attack.

There was a scraping, scuttling noise below her and Rosie looked down just in time to see a weasel and a stoat scrambling up the trunk. Their mouths opened in a snarl and she could see the rows of sharp little teeth, but she held tight to the tree and kicked at them.

Her foot caught the weasel full on its snout and it lost its grip and fell. The kick only brushed the stoat, though, and it leaped from the tree on to her leg. She felt its claws dig through her jeans into her skin as it ran up her leg. She punched downwards with her fist and knocked it off her knee. It rolled and tumbled in the air and crashed down next to the alligator.

All the animals looked at each other as if to see which of them would be the next to attack, but none of them moved. Rosie felt hope rise in her – perhaps she had scared them off.

Then the wolf lifted its head and began to howl. The fox started to bark. The owl hooted. The stoat and the weasel stood on their hind legs and hissed. Even the alligator added to the noise by slapping its tail against the tree.

For a moment Rosie didn't understand what they were doing. Then she realized: they were sending a signal. And it was a signal that had been heard.

'Well, my little ones, have you found her?' called a familiar voice from the road.

It was the Djinn.

Chapter Twenty-one

The animals stopped their calls and turned to watch as the Djinn walked through the wood towards them. When he was directly under the tree he looked up and Rosie could see that his face was becoming more and more like a reptile's. His skin was even beginning to have snake-like patterns across it.

'Well,' he hissed from his thin lips, 'if you don't want to join us by choice, you must be *forced* to join us.'

He pointed his finger at some ivy that was growing at the base of the oak tree. At once the ivy stem began to snake upwards, twisting round and round the tree. Before Rosie could do anything it had reached her, wrapping itself across her legs and arms and pinning her against the trunk of the tree.

There was a flash of lightning close by and, as the thunder rumbled and rolled across the sky, the Djinn got hold of the ivy and climbed up towards her. Rosie wriggled wildly to try to free herself, but the ivy only tightened its grip on her.

'There's no escape,' the Djinn sneered as he drew level with her, 'so don't waste time struggling.

Now then, take this back.'

He held out the parcel and Rosie could see that his hands were green and webbed like a lizard's.

She shook her head and clenched her fists so that he couldn't put the Djinn Star into her hand.

'Take it!' he shouted, and pressed the parcel against her fist.

Rosie shook her head again and suddenly she saw a flicker in those cold, serpent eyes. He was afraid. He was scared that he wouldn't be able to make her take the Star. She felt a moment of hope, but a new look came into the Djinn's eyes – a cruel, savage look.

He pointed at the ivy again and it began to wind round her wrists, tighter and tighter.

'Open your hands!' he yelled.

'No,' Rosie said, trying not to let him see how much it hurt.

The ivy squeezed harder, cutting into her wrists and stopping the blood from reaching her hands. Already her fingers were tingling and cold and her arm muscles felt weak. The suckers on the ivy were biting into her skin as if they were trying to suck her blood.

'Take the Star,' the Djinn ordered.

Rosie clenched her teeth together to stop herself crying out in pain, and shook her head.

The Djinn pointed his finger again and a branch of the ivy whipped upwards, coiling round the tree and twining itself round her neck. It jerked tight and began to choke her. In a few seconds her face was burning and her lungs screamed for air.

She would have to open her hand and let the Djinn give her the parcel. She couldn't hold out any longer.

She must have air.

Her eyes were growing dim. And now there was a ringing in her ears.

Dong. Dong. Dong.

It must be a funeral bell.

Dong. Dong. Dong.

Perhaps she was already dead. It was her funeral.

A silly rhyme came into her head:

> *The bells of hell*
> *Go ting-a-ling-a-ling.*

But these bells were going: dong, dong, dong. They weren't the bells of hell. They weren't funeral bells either.

They were the chimes of the church clock.

Dong. Dong. Dong.

That made twelve chimes.

It was midnight.

There was a scream from the Djinn.

Rosie opened her eyes and saw him scrambling down the tree trunk to the ground.

The ivy stopped squeezing and quickly unwound itself from her throat and shrank back to its original size. The creatures round the base of the tree all took one pace forward as if trying to escape and then froze. The magic had left them and they had become stuffed animals again – stiff, lifeless and sad.

Rosie took a deep, deep breath, but her head was still spinning from lack of air and she could feel herself swaying. She reached out to grab a branch to steady herself but her hand closed round nothing.

She fell head first out of the tree.

Chapter Twenty-two

Rosie fell.

She waited for the crash on to the hard ground, but instead there was a gentle bump and she found herself lying in a pair of strong, hairy arms. It was Sidri.

'Well done, Wosie,' he said, gently putting her down on her feet. 'You did it!'

'Did what?' Rosie asked, feeling her legs wobble under her.

'You resisted the Djinn and became a real human being, my dear,' said Mr Ikbal, appearing by her side and taking hold of her hand to steady her as her legs nearly gave way. 'You resisted temptation and you resisted threats – not many people can do that. You did very well. In fact, you *both* did very well.'

He smiled at his young helper and patted him on the head. 'Yes, young Sidri, I'm proud of you too. The way you dashed into that house to fight the Djinn and help Rosie showed that you have the makings of a first-class Finder. I think you can safely assume that you have passed your first mission with flying colours.'

Sidri's crocodiley face blushed pink with

pleasure. He looked at Rosie and smiled shyly.

'And now that it is midnight,' Mr Ikbal went on, 'we can send this one back to the other side.'

He pointed to the Djinn, who was standing, frozen in mid-step, with his face towards them. Even though he wasn't moving, he seemed to stare at Rosie with an expression that was filled with so much anger and hatred that a chill ran through her.

'My name is Ikbal. I arrest you in my name; in the name of my young apprentice, Sidri; in the name of our young friend, Rosie, and in the ninety-nine names of goodness. You have been captured and I send you back to where you belong.'

Mr Ikbal raised both his hands. The Djinn took a small step towards them and disappeared. It all happened so quickly that Rosie couldn't believe her eyes.

'Where's he gone?' she said, ducking behind Mr Ikbal in case the Djinn reappeared and tried to catch her again.

'To the other side,' Mr Ikbal said. 'And don't worry, this time we'll keep a close eye on him and make sure he doesn't slip over here and cause trouble again.'

'Where exactly is "the other side"?' Rosie asked.

'There,' Mr Ikbal and Sidri said together. But when she looked, they were both pointing in opposite directions.

Mr Ikbal laughed and said, 'I'm afraid it's rather

confusing. You see, it's everywhere – except here, of course. Oh dear, that doesn't help, does it? How can I explain? Imagine that the world you see all around you is only a room in a house. You can only see this room, but if you could go through the door you would find that there are many rooms. And yet all the rooms are in the same house.'

'But where's the door?' Rosie asked, trying hard to understand.

'Here.' Sidri took one step forward and disappeared. A moment later, he was back again. 'See?' he said brightly.

'Can I go through the door too?' Rosie asked.

'I'm afraid not. Not yet, ' Mr Ikbal said. 'Human beings have to stay here.'

'I wish I'd become a Djinn, then,' Rosie said, thinking how good it would have been to do magic, and fly, and go to the other side.

'Oh, my dear, you don't mean that – look how bravely you fought against it. A caterpillar doesn't want to turn into a worm just because a worm is longer and can dig holes in the ground. Oh no – a caterpillar knows that it must concentrate on being a proper caterpillar because, somewhere deep inside, it knows that one day it will turn into a butterfly.'

While Mr Ikbal was speaking, Rosie had been staring at the place where the Djinn had disappeared, but now she realized that the whole area was lit up by a bright light.

She turned her head and saw two shimmering

figures floating in the air.

'Oh, Mr Ikbal, Sidri – you're . . . you're beautiful.'

It was the only word she could think of, but it wasn't good enough to describe the wonder and happiness she felt, looking at them.

Silver rays of light sparkled off them and they glowed with fun and gentleness and laughter and kindness and wisdom.

'So beautiful,' she murmured. 'You really are angels.'

'We are what we have always been – it is you who have changed,' said Mr Ikbal. 'Before, you were seeing us with the eyes of a Djinn, but now the goodness in you sees something else.'

'Oh no,' Rosie gasped, 'you're fading. I can see right through you.'

'We have to go, my dear.'

'No, don't,' she cried. 'Please stay – you're . . . you're my friends.'

The fast-fading figure of Sidri floated over to her and wrapped shining wings round her.

'I'll always be your friend,' Sidri whispered.

He gave her a hug that sent light tingling right to the centre of her heart.

'Come, Sidri, we must go,' Mr Ikbal said. 'And remember, Rosie – we are like the air you breathe: you cannot see us or touch us, but we are always here.'

Rosie watched as they grew dimmer and dimmer.

Even when they had gone she stayed there, staring at where they had been, with the ghost of their brightness in her eyes and the light from Sidri's hug still tingling in her heart.

Rosie would never forget those moments.

On the long ride back home through the countryside lit up by a bright moon; during the following day while she waited for her family to come home – she kept thinking of the shimmering beauty of her two angels.

And when she felt the softness of her mum's kiss and the warmth of her dad's hug, when she saw the cheeky smile on Mark's face, and when Jimmy held out his trusting little arms to her, it was almost as if she could see Mr Ikbal and Sidri again.

She never said anything to her mum and dad, of course, because she knew it would be too hard to explain. But, a few days later, there was a storm. The wind whipped the last of the brown leaves from the trees and it was raining too hard to go out in the garden, so Mark asked her to make up a story for him.

Rosie decided to tell him about the Finders.

She changed everybody's name so that he wouldn't guess it was a true story, but she told him everything, starting from that day when she got up, on what seemed an ordinary morning, and went down to breakfast . . .

It took hours to tell the story, but Mark listened all the way through without a word and at the end, when Rosie told him about how the Finders faded away, there were tears in his eyes.

'I wish they could be real – the Finders – don't you?' he said, staring at the fire.

Rosie nodded.

There was a long silence, then he went on.

'I think they are real but we just can't see them. I bet there are millions of things we can't see.'

He got up and walked to the door.

'Anyway,' he said as he opened the door and turned back to her, 'I know they're real because I've seen them.'

'Where?' laughed Rosie.

'In your eyes when you were telling the story. I could see them as bright as anything. They sort of smiled at me all the time. They looked nice.'

He stood for a moment, as if thinking about what he had just said, then he went out and closed the door.